MYTHS
— AND —
LEGENDS

MYTHS
AND
LEGENDS

FROM CHEROKEE DANCES
TO VOODOO TRANCES

JOHN PEMBERTON

CHARTWELL
BOOKS

CONTENTS

PART 2: AFRICA & THE MIDDLE EAST

ANCIENT EGYPT

THE MIDDLE EAST

SUB-SAHARAN AFRICA

OTHER AFRICAN MYTHOLOGY

PART 3: THE AMERICAS

PART 4: ASIA & OCEANIA

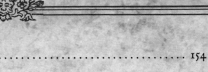

INTRODUCTION

The impulse to create myths seems to be inherent in all cultures, uniting peoples from every corner of the Earth and from every period of human history. That the stories gathered together in this book have survived to the present day is testament to the importance our predecessors placed upon them. The authors and custodians of these works valued them as highly as any treasure, protected them as fiercely as any territory or ruler. Across the ages, humankind has sung these sacred words by camp fires and gravesides, carved them in tombs and temples, recited and re-enacted them at festivals and ceremonies, and scratched them with quills on papyrus, vellum and paper.

Many of the cultures that produced these works have themselves long since vanished but, through the myths and legends presented here, the gods and demons that sprang from their imaginations – and maybe even their realities – live on.

WHAT IS A MYTH – AND WHAT IS A LEGEND?

Though it was the ancient Greeks who gave us the word we use to describe these stories mythos, myths themselves did not begin with the Greeks, and many of the narratives collected here predate them by several centuries. Indeed, it is probable that myths are as old as human thought itself, inspired by the desire to answer such universal questions as 'where did we come from?' and 'what happens when we die?'.

Myths and legends, then, offer a way of understanding the world through metaphor and analogy. The meanings of myths can change according to the cultural beliefs of the reader, but the questions they seek to answer remain the same, which is why so many common themes recur in tales that are separated by thousands of years and thousands of miles. Many of the similarities in the myths are highlighted throughout this book, though readers will doubtless find many more of their own.

Academics divide stories of the imagination into categories such as myth, legend and folklore, in order to distinguish between the vast array of tales that have been created by humankind. In truth, all such categories are fluid and likely to overlap at times. Myths tend to deal with the unknown and the supernatural, whilst legends tend to relate to the lives and achievements of real-life individuals, and folklore often focusses on aspects of morality. Many stories, however, refuse to sit neatly within one particular rigid definition, weaving historical fact with invention or exaggeration, melding real events and locations with imagined plots and fabled dreamlands. That countless stories from the world's great religions appear also (albeit often in modified form) in the canon of mythology only adds to the difficulty of categorization.

This book seeks to gather as wide a collection of stories as is reasonably possible within the confines of a single volume, and purists may thus find that some of the tales included here lie beyond a strict definition of either myth or legend. The author will be content if readers simply discover stories that are new to them, or rediscover stories that were familiar to them only in part. The intention is to kindle an interest in these remarkable tales, in the belief that readers whose thirst has been whetted will seek out for themselves further resources that relate to the fields that interest them the most.

The narratives in this collection have thus been selected in order to amaze, intrigue and delight, as well as educate and inform. For, when all is said and done, the ancient authors of the myths and legends themselves must surely have had that same aim in mind.

COMMON THEMES

Myths and legends reflect our collective dreams and fears, reminding us of the shared experiences that unite us as a species. The characters and settings of the stories in this collection vary widely, yet beneath the surface many common patterns emerge. In this sense, myths represent the 'collective unconscious' posited by Carl Jung, tackling themes that are universal and eternal. Jung identified certain archetypes that recur in

almost all myths, allowing peoples from very different cultures to find some mirror of their own selves in the characters portrayed.

It is certainly true that most modern readers will be able to instantly identify with the heroes and villains of these tales, and recognize in their stories dilemmas and questions which still trouble humankind today. For hidden somewhere within these fabled histories and outlandish prophecies, these tales of epic heroes and treacherous villains, this litany of mighty gods and fearsome monsters; somewhere within these soaring dreams and lonely nightmares lies our best collective attempt to answer the question of what it means to be human.

CREATION AND DESTRUCTION

Perhaps the greatest single mystery for ancient human beings was the question of how the world began, and the associated question of where human beings first came from. Almost all cultures have some explanation for the events that occurred before the arrival of humankind. Most focus on a benevolent 'creator god' fashioning humans from clay, wood or some other natural material, and frequently separate processes are described for the construction of men and women.

Often destruction appears hand in hand with creation, as angry gods destroy early or unfinished versions of humans. Tales of floods can be found from every corner of the Earth, leading some to suggest that they may all relate to a single real world event. We will probably never know the truth behind such stories, but the reader cannot fail to spot the astonishing similarity between many flood myths from the disparate cultures represented here. In all versions of the story, the destruction wrought is catastrophic, and threatens the

ABOVE: Parthenon, Athens, Greece.

very future of humankind – though in most cases one or two virtuous individuals are preselected to survive and propagate the species.

DEATH AND UNDERWORLD

Closely linked to the ubiquitous creation myths are tales about how death first appeared in the world, and what happens to humans when they die. A common motif is the idea that humans were originally godlike, immortal, and living in some form of paradise. Humanity's 'fall' takes different forms – sometimes it is an act of disobedience – as in the myth of *The Two Trees from Micronesia* – and sometimes it is pure bad luck – as in the African myth of *The Chameleon*, but the result is always the same. Human beings become mortal, and the pain of losing a loved one is introduced to the world for the very first time.

As to what happens to the departed, most cultures have a separate spirit realm for the good and the evil – a paradise and an underworld. For the ancient Egyptians it was necessary to negotiate the latter in order to reach the former, whilst in many other myths the gods, or a gatekeeper acting on behalf of them, would choose in which of the realms the departed would spend eternity. In many cultures it was believed that the dead could return, to console, advise or terrorize the living. What is shared across all myths is the belief that death is not the end of existence, but merely a different realm that the living cannot reach.

HEROES AND QUESTS

Heroes come in many different shapes and sizes, but almost all are male, and mortal rather than divine. Indeed it is the flaws within heroes that makes their stories so compelling, and allows the reader to share in the triumphs and disasters of the hero's journey. Often the hero has some special power – either an object given to them by a supernatural deity, or a natural attribute derived from a divine lineage (heroes who are half-mortal and half-god are commonplace).

In many myths, a hero arrives to save a culture, vanquish a demon, or monster, bring a new gift (fire is a recurring motif), or lead a people to some new promised land. Heroes are frequently depicted as great teachers, providing humankind with the skills to hunt, fish, heal, or set down their thoughts in writing. The births of many of the first great civilizations are attributed to heroes who excel at construction, or at leading armies in triumphant battles.

In quests, heroes are given seemingly impossible tasks and undertake perilous

ABOVE: Close-up of a float embroidered with a mask of a female demon, Takayama festival, Japan.

journeys to find a sacred object or defeat a fearsome foe. The hero is tested to breaking point, and often requires outside assistance to achieve his goal. Love is perhaps the most common motivation, but glory and duty are also recurrent themes. Fate and destiny almost always result in the hero triumphing, though often at some significant cost.

Of all the similarities between the myths of cultures separated by vast geographical and historical distance, perhaps the most striking is that of a 'hero quest' to the underworld. Stories of journeys to a land of the dead appear in the mythologies of almost all ancient cultures, illustrating that for as long as humankind has had to face mortality, it has also sought to conquer death and make contact with those who have been taken from the land of the living.

TRICKSTER FIGURES

One clearly identifiable archetype that makes an appearance in many mythologies is the 'trickster', someone or something that breaks the normal rules of behaviour. Often the trickster is a deity, such as Loki in Norse myth, but just as often she or he is a type of hero, such as Blue Jay in Native American myth. Tricksters can be wise or foolish, and their mischief can be deliberate or accidental. Ultimately, however, their trickery tends to produce positive results, either for themselves or for humanity in general. The tricks they play teach human beings valuable lessons, whilst also reminding them of the capricious nature of the universe.

Frequently tricksters are also shape-shifters, capable of taking on many different forms, and also of changing gender. They are often presented as comic characters, though the tasks they undertake may be sacred or sombre.

STRUCTURE AND SOURCES

This book groups the world's myths into four geographical regions in order to provide an easy-to-follow structure for the reader. Myths from neighbouring countries often share distinct similarities, but it should be noted that many of the cultures featured here were separated by vast periods of time, even though they may have been close to one another upon a map. Approximate dates are provided wherever possible in order to help the reader distinguish between myths of different periods, though in many cases historians can only guess at the real age of a belief system. Some tales can be dated from their linguistic style or from references within the text, but in most cases we can only be sure of the date of the earliest written source of the myth. Since the vast majority of myths were passed down orally before the widespread adoption of writing, it is likely that some of the myths collected here are many thousands of years older than the official written sources.

It is also important to point out that explorers, missionaries, and conquering armies are responsible for many of the written accounts of past cultures' belief systems. These settlers often had their own agenda, and their own prejudices regarding the cultures they reported upon. Stories may thus have been distorted, exaggerated, or misunderstood.

Language, too, evolves and changes over time, and this often results in the same mythological figure having several different names, spelt in slightly different ways. This book uses the most widely accepted spellings for the names of characters and stories, and indicates the most frequently used alternative names or spellings that the reader is likely to encounter.

PART 1
EUROPE

Before the advent of Christianity, Europe was a place ruled by strange and capricious gods who seemed to toy with mankind for their sport. In their desperate attempt to make sense of an often cruel world, the Europeans devised a pantheon of deities and mythical creatures who did endless battle across the skies, the Earth and the underworld. Great heroes set off on daring adventures and undertook seemingly impossible challenges in order to find love, peace and immortality. European mythology is a treasure trove of some of the best known and best loved stories of all time, which resonate in the minds of modern readers due to their eternal themes and unforgettable characters.

THE ANCIENT GREEKS

The birthplace of Western civilization, the ancient Greek Empire flourished from the 8th century BCE until its conquest by the Romans in 146 BCE. Because the Greeks placed such a high value on the written word, many of their most ancient myths have survived almost completely intact.

The Greeks were the first to dramatize stories for performance on the stage, and also gave us the word we still use to describe epic and universal tales - myths, from the Greek word mythos. Astronomers still use the names of ancient Greek deities to describe many of the most important celestial bodies we see in the sky today.

The Greek myths are vivid tales of love, death, and adventure which to this day still have the power to thrill, delight, and amaze the reader.

THE GREEK CREATION MYTH

The story of creation was first set down in *Theogony*, a poem attributed to the writer Hesiod, which was composed around 700 BCE. From chaos sprang forth Eros (the force of love and desire), Gaia (the Earth) and Tartarus (the underworld), followed by Nyx (the night) and Erebus (darkness).

Gaia then gave birth to Ourea (the mountains), Ouranos (the sky, the heavens), and Pontus (the sea). Erebus and Nyx created Aither (brightness) and Hemera (the daytime).

A DARK TURN

It is at this point that the creation myth takes a turn for the worse. Ouranos embraces Gaia every night, and their union creates numerous children, three of whom so physically disgust Ouranos that he banishes them to Tartarus. Their mother Gaia then conspires with her other children to overthrow Ouranos, and he is castrated with a sickle by his son Cronos, the youngest of the brood. Cronos throws his father's genitals into the ocean, where they cause the sea to foam and create Aphrodite, the goddess of love.

One version of the creation myth has the goddess Eurynome (closely associated with Oceanid, the 'daughter of the Ocean') initially ruling over the universe. Eurynome mates with Ophion, a sea serpent, in order to produce Eros. In some versions Eurynome mates with the North Wind.

THE BIRTH OF ZEUS

Cronos is so concerned that his own children might in turn overthrow him in the way he did his father, that whenever his wife Rhea gives birth to a child, he eats it. Rhea tricks Cronos by hiding their child Zeus and wrapping a stone in a baby's blanket, which Cronos then eats, believing it to be his child. Zeus is smuggled away to a cave on Mount Ida in Crete, where he is raised in safety by his grandmother Gaia. In other versions he is raised by a goat, a nymph or a shepherd.

THE GOD OF THUNDER

When Zeus grows up he feeds his father a magical potion, causing Cronos to vomit up all of the children that he had previously swallowed. He then frees the brothers of Cronos from their prison in Tartarus, the underworld. Zeus receives the power of thunder as a reward for all the good that he has done and the brothers and children of Cronos join Zeus in doing battle with Cronos and his titans, and ultimately manage to defeat them and banish Cronos to the underworld of Tartarus. Atlas, one of the titans who fought against Zeus, is punished by having to hold up the sky forever more.

Zeus then becomes king of the gods and divides the world with his brothers Poseidon and Hades, by drawing lots. Zeus draws the sky, Poseidon the oceans and Hades the underworld.

Zeus is the most important of all of the Greek gods, and is depicted with a thunderbolt to signify his role as god of thunder and the sky.

THE ODYSSEY

The very word odyssey has come to mean an epic quest, and that is what the original poem, written by Homer circa 700 BCE, delivers. It is over 12,000 lines long and charts the journey home of Odysseus, a hero whose earlier exploits in the Trojan War are described in Homer's other epic poem *The Iliad*.

NYMPHS AND GIANTS

Odysseus tells the story of his adventures to King Alcinos of Phaeacia. On return from being shipwrecked on the island of Scherie whilst escaping from the nymph, Calypso, who had previously imprisoned him on her island, Ogygia, Odysseus tells the King how he travelled to the land of the Lotus Eaters, where the inhabitants dined only on lotus flowers that made them sleepy and apathetic. Here Odysseus lost three of his comrades who had decided to try the flower and had fallen into the island's trance. Odysseus set sail again but was then captured by a Cyclops, a giant with one single eye in the centre of its forehead, on the island of the Cyclopes. Trapped in the Cyclops's cave with a herd of sheep, Odysseus and his men escaped by blinding the Cyclops and then tying themselves to the bellies of the sheep so that the Cyclops couldn't feel them as they passed through the exit of the cave.

SO CLOSE YET SO FAR

Next Odysseus met Aeolus, the ruler of the winds, who gave him a bag which contained all of the winds – except the west wind – which, by partially opening would give Odysseus a steady breeze to help blow his ship home. However, his crew opened the bag fully, thinking it was treasure, and a hurricane was released which blew them onto the island of a witch called Circe. She turned all the men into pigs, but Odysseus managed to free them from her spell with the help of Hermes, a messenger from the gods. From here Odysseus and his men journeyed on to the edge of the world, where the spirit of Odysseus's mother told him of the trouble that awaited him on his return home. She told him that his home was besieged by suitors to his wife Penelope, as it was believed that Odysseus had died at war. The suitors were also plotting to kill Odysseus's son Telemachus and rule in his place.

SIRENS AND SEA MONSTERS

Odysseus and his crew managed to avoid falling victim to the sirens – who lulled sailors to their deaths with beautiful songs – by filling their ears with wax. They then passed between the great sea monsters of Scylla and Charybdis and land on the island of Thrinacia. Here the crew killed the sacred cattle of the sun god Helios, who, with the help of one of Zeus's thunderbolts, cursed them with a shipwreck in which all but Odysseus are drowned. Odysseus washed ashore on the island of Calypso, where he was kept prisoner for seven years.

After relating his story to King Alcinos, Odysseus is given a ship with a crew of Phaeacian sailors and he returns home. Disguising himself as a beggar in order to secretly discover how things now stand in his household, he visits the hut of Eumaeus,

LEFT: Illustration of Phidias's statue in gold and ivory of the Olympian, Zeus.

a swineherd and one of his former slaves. Although Eumaeus does not recognize Odysseus, he treats him well, providing him with food and shelter despite his lowly appearance. Odysseus returns to his own home with that faithful Eumaeus in tow, in order to observe the behaviour of the suitors who now dwell there. He is still recognized by no one, but in one of the myth's most poignant moments, his faithful dog Argos lifts his head and wags his tail as Odysseus approaches. Neglected during the twenty years that Odysseus has been away, the dog is close to death and does not have the strength to get to his feet, but the fact that he manages to remember his master causes Odysseus to shed a tear.

DIVINE INTERVENTION

With the help of some divine intervention from Zeus's daughter Athena – who had always had a soft spot for Odysseus, he finally manages to meet up with his son Telemachus. Athena gives Odysseus a helping hand by restoring and enhancing his appearance so that Telemachus would believe him to be a god. Odysseus enters his home to find the suitors there behaving in a rowdy and dishonourable fashion. Together Odysseus and Telemachus kill the suitors at Odysseus's home and Odysseus is reunited with his wife Penelope.

ABOVE: *Odysseus and the Sirens*, Herbert James Draper, 1909.

JASON AND THE GOLDEN FLEECE

Jason was the son of Aeson, the rightful king of Iolcus (a city in Thessaly). Aeson was overthrown by his half-brother Pelias, who swore that he would relinquish the throne if Jason could retrieve the Golden Fleece and bring it to him. The Golden Fleece (which had once belonged to Zeus) was the fleece of a precious winged, gold-haired ram and it hung from an oak tree in a sacred grove where it was guarded by a dragon that never slept. Jason set forth on the ship Argo, with a crew of heroes known as 'the Argonauts', in order to find the Golden Fleece and take his rightful place on the throne of Iolcus.

ARGONAUTICA

The ensuing quest of Jason and his Argonauts (thought to number around 50) is told in the epic Greek poem Argonautica, written by Apollonius in the 3rd century BCE, although the original story was known to the Greeks some five centuries earlier. It is set in the time of the Trojan War, around 1300 BCE. The story is an epic tale of adventure, with incidents and locations too numerous to list in full, as Jason journeys to find the fleece, which hung at Aia in the land of Colchis, a place the Greeks would have considered to be the edge of the known world. Along the way certain key encounters prove crucial in helping Jason to complete his task.

THE CURSE OF APHRODITE

Jason first arrives at the island of Lemnos, in the Aegean sea. The women of the island had all murdered their husbands after being cursed by Aphrodite – the goddess of love, beauty, and sexuality – for not worshipping her shrines. Jason and his argonauts breed with the women in order to repopulate the island and Jason fathers twin sons, Euneus and Thoas, with the queen, Hypsipyle.

Soon after, Jason loses his chief Argonaut, Heracles, who fails to return to the ship after going in search of a fellow Argonaut who had been carried off by nymphs whilst seeking water. They then rescue the blind prophet Phineus from the winged harpies who had been tormenting him. Phineus predicts that Jason will be the first to successfully navigate the 'clashing rocks' which guard the entrance to the Black Sea. This Jason duly does, and he reaches the land of Colchis. He asks King Aietes, custodian of the fleece, to hand it to him, and Aietes agrees if Jason can complete certain challenges. First he must harness two fire-breathing bulls, then he must plough the Field of Ares and sow the field with dragons' teeth.

MEDEA AND THE DRAGON

Aphrodite orders Eros to make Medea, the daughter of King Aietes, and Jason fall in love. Knowing that her father intends to kill Jason, Medea then offers to help him with the challenges as long as he will marry her. When Jason agrees, Medea provides him with a lotion that protects him from the fire-breathing bulls. After ploughing the field and sowing the dragons' teeth, phantom warriors spring from the earth, but Jason causes them to fight amongst themselves until none are left. King Aietes still refuses to hand over the fleece, and so Medea takes Jason to the sacred grove and lulls to sleep the dragon that guards the fleece. With the fleece in their possession, they flee back to the ship and journey home.

BROKEN PROMISE

Back at Iolcus, Jason discovers that King Pelias has killed his father, Aeson, and that as a result his mother has died of grief. In vengeance Medea tricks the daughters of Pelias into killing their father.

Jason and Medea place the golden fleece in the temple of Zeus, then journey to Corinth, where Medea reclaims the throne that was rightfully hers. She and Jason rule for ten years, until Jason, who becomes power hungry, betrays her by seeking to marry the king of Thebes's daughter, Glauce in order to strengthen his political allegiance.

MEDEA'S REVENGE

Medea, heartbroken when she finds out that it was not true love but a spell by Aphrodite, takes revenge by sending Glauce a wedding dress made of poison. As soon as Glauce puts the dress on it sticks to her body and burns her to death. Medea, who is still full of wrath, goes on to kill the children that she had with Jason. Jason's infidelity infuriates the goddess of women and marriage, Hera, and she ensures he dies a sad and lonely man.

ABOVE: Jason with the stolen Golden Fleece on his shoulder.

ORPHEUS IN THE UNDERWORLD

Orpheus was known as a fine poet and musician, excelling in particular with the lyre – a stringed instrument like a small U-shaped harp. Such was their beauty, his songs and tunes could make birds, animals and even nature itself dance. His lyre was made of gold, and was given to him by Apollo, the god of music and son of Zeus. Orpheus travelled with Jason as one of the Argonauts, but he is best known for his journey into the underworld, in pursuit of his dead wife Eurydice.

Eurydice dies after being bitten on the heel by a venomous snake. The grief-stricken Orpheus plays a mournful tune so beautiful that it melts even the hearts of Hades and Persephone, the deities that govern the underworld. They grant him his wish to take Eurydice back to the world of the living, on condition that he walks in front of her and does not look back. The lovers set off, but as soon as Orpheus reaches the upper world, he glances back to ensure that Eurydice is still with him. As soon as he does so, she disappears back into the underworld forever.

From then on Orpheus forswears the love of women, taking only young men as lovers. Enraged by Orpheus' rejection, a group of women who were followers of Dionysus tear him to pieces in a wine-fuelled frenzy. His severed head and lyre float down the river Hebrus - still singing mournful songs as it goes.

Similar journeys into the underworld occur in myths and legends across the world, as we shall see.

ABOVE: Orpheus, a musician from Greek mythology, charms Hades and Persephone, king and queen of the Underworld, with his lyre playing in order to win back his dead wife Eurydice, circa 1200 BCE.

PANDORA'S BOX

In Greek mythology Pandora was the first woman, created from clay by Hephaestus, the god of craftsmen and sculptors. Hephaestus was acting under instruction from Zeus, who was angered that Prometheus had stolen the gift of fire and given it to mankind. Zeus then instructs all the other gods and goddesses to give her traits and characteristics that could go on to make mankind's life harder, before giving her to Prometheus' brother Epimetheus as a gift, and he accepts her, despite his brother's warnings.

Famously, Pandora goes on to open a box containing all of the world's evils, which are then unleashed upon mankind. All that remains in the box is hope, which she keeps inside by resealing the lid. Exactly what sort of evils were in the box, and exactly how she came into possession of the box, is not clear – different versions of the myth offer different explanations. In one version, Pandora is given the box as a wedding present when she marries Epimetheus. In another version she finds the box. In the early versions of the myth the box was actually a jar or jug, and the word box seems to have been introduced into the story as the result of a mistranslation.

CURIOSITY VERSUS HOPE

It is not clear if hope, the only thing left in the box, is being preserved for or kept away from humankind – as with so many myths, there are numerous different interpretations of the message. Indeed some scholars argue that it was expectation rather than hope that remained – again the original Greek word can be translated in either way. Whether the story has a comforting or desolate ending thus depends on how you read it, but either way it shows the effect that the very human trait of curiosity can have – but whatever happens we still have the hope of hope.

THE EVILS OF WOMAN?

Most cultures have stories which attempt to explain how evil came into the world. There are clear parallels with the Bible story of Eve, another female, who bit into the forbidden fruit and caused humankind to be expelled from the Garden of Eden. Feminist translations of these stories describe them as a mysogynist's depiction of female sexuality. Pandora's box is sometimes seen as the female womb, and the evils released from it depict the unease that the society of the time had with female sexuality. Maybe the hope left in the box was a symbol of the male form.

ABOVE: According to Greek mythology Pandora was the first woman on Earth, created by the god Hephaestus at the request of the god Zeus.

THESEUS AND THE MINOTAUR

The Athenians, having lost a war with King Minos of Crete, were obliged to send him seven boys and seven girls every nine years, so that they could be devoured by the Minotaur – a monster which was half man and half bull, that was housed within a vast labyrinth.

LOVE AT FIRST SIGHT

Theseus, the founder-king of Athens, vows to kill the Minotaur and so volunteers to take the place of one of the boys, and upon arrival in Crete meets Minos's daughter, Ariadne. Ariadne falls in love immediately with Theseus and gives him a sword, and a ball of red yarn that she had been spinning, to help him with his task. Ariadne then goes on to tell Theseus how to find the Minotaur, as she has been given instructions by the labyrinth's creator, Daedalus. Theseus heads off into the labyrinth but first ties one end of the yarn to the labyrinth's entrance so that he can find his way back out. Theseus finds the Minotaur sleeping and, after an epic battle, manages to slay it and escape from the labyrinth.

ABANDONMENT

For the help granted by Ariadne, Theseus had pledged to take her to be his wife, but abandons her on the way home. She curses him by changing the sail of his ship from white to black. Theseus had told his father Aegeus he would return with a white sail if he was successful in slaying the Minotaur. Seeing the black sail, Aegeus assumes his son has been killed and he commits suicide by throwing himself into the sea.

RIGHT: A pelike depicting Theseus and the Minotaur, painted by the Syleus Painter, circa 470-460 BCE.

ICARUS

Icarus and his father Daedalus were imprisoned on the island of Crete by King Minos for the part Daedalus played in helping Theseus defeat the Minotaur. Whilst imprisoned Daedalus creates two pairs of wings, made from feathers and wax, in order for him and his son to escape. He warns Icarus not to fly too close to the sun or too close to the sea as they make their escape. Icarus ignores his father's advice, and exhilarated with his new-found ability to fly, flies too close to the sun, melting his wings. Flapping his bare arms to no avail, he falls into the sea which now bears his name (the Icarian Sea) and is killed.

THE HUMAN CONDITION

There are many morals that can be taken from this story. As a story for children it touches on the importance of listening to your elders, and it was probably also used to portray the fragility of the human condition. Icarus flew so high and close to the sun – a place associated with the gods – and somewhere that he did not belong. His punishment for this was to fall to his death, to the bottom of the sea, which shows that humans should know their place in the spiritual world.

ABOVE: Icarus, the son of Daedalus from Greek mythology tries to escape from imprisonment on Crete using wings made of wax and feathers, circa 1300 BCE.

ATLANTIS

Generations have been fascinated by the story of Atlantis, the legendary island that sank without trace beneath the sea. It remains a staple of sci-fi writers to this day, and even featured as a location in the massively popular video game *Tomb Raider*.

It was Plato who first described Atlantis (or the 'isle of Atlas') in around 360 BCE, claiming it lay 'in front of the pillars of Hercules' and had disappeared over 9,000 years earlier. Plato talks of a civilization that was highly advanced for its time, building great cities linked to the coast by miles of canals. Many parts of Western Europe were supposedly conquered by its mighty navy. Shortly after the Atlanteans attempted, unsuccessfully, to invade Athens, however, the entire island was wiped off the map by a massive earthquake 'in a single day and night of misfortune'.

No one has ever conclusively identified the location of Atlantis, though plenty have tried. Sites across the Mediterranean and Atlantic oceans have been suggested, along with locations as distant as Sweden, Cuba, and India. The majority of historical experts think it never existed at all, as Plato is the only person to mention the island, and he was writing long after the supposed disaster. Whether it existed or not, the story of the advanced civilization that disappeared forever in a single day seems to have resonated throughout the ages, and there are parallels in tales of catastrophic floods in myths all around the world. The legendary lost Celtic islands of Lyonnesse, Ys, and Cantre'r Gwaelod (see page 51) also have striking similarities with Atlantis.

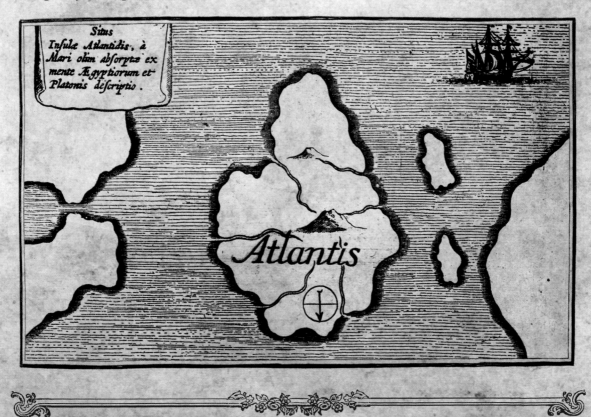

ABOVE: An illustration from a book published in Germany entitled, *Land Sila and Air* showing a map of the island of Atlantis, circa 1600.

THE ANCIENT ROMANS

The Romans appropriated many of their myths from other cultures – principally the Greeks – but they also had their own pantheon of gods, and many of these had highly detailed histories which were set down by great Roman poets such as Virgil, Ovid, and Horace. As the mighty Roman Empire spread, additional myths from conquered lands were assimilated into the Roman belief system and archaeological evidence suggests that the Romans were quite happy to worship numerous gods side by side. A highly ritualistic society, the Romans would pray to whichever god seemed best suited to their particular needs.

ROMULUS AND REMUS

The story of Romulus and Remus is a type of 'creation myth' for the city of Rome. The two boys were the twin sons of the god Mars, but Mars abandons them on the banks of the river Tiber. There they are found by a she-wolf, who feeds them on her milk. Later a shepherd adopts the boys and raises them as his own sons.

FOUNDATIONS OF AN EMPIRE

When Romulus and Remus grow up, they decide to found a city on the spot where the shepherd had discovered them. In an argument over who should rule the city, Romulus kills his brother and thus becomes the first ruler of the city. The new city is named Roma, after him. Romulus invites all those who want a second chance at life to join him in the city, and thus the first inhabitants include many exiles, criminals, and runaway slaves. Noticing a shortage of women, Romulus invites a neighbouring tribe, the Sabines, to Rome for a festival. He captures many of their women in order to populate Rome. After many fierce battles, the Sabines and Romans make peace and live side by side in peace.

Romulus ruled Rome for 37 years, whereupon he disappeared. The Roman myth tells that he was taken up into the sky by a whirlwind, but there are also some suspicions that he was assassinated by members of the Senate who became frustrated at the authoritarian nature of his rule.

LUCRETIA

Experts believe Lucretia was a real person, rather than a mythological character, but her story has since passed into the realm of legend and inspired numerous other artists and authors, including Shakespeare, whose poem *The Rape Of Lucrece* is based upon the Roman tale. It is noteworthy because it led directly to the overthrow of the Roman monarchy and the establishment of the Roman republic. The death of Lucretia is believed to have occurred around 508 BCE.

Lucretia, the chaste wife of the Roman governor, Collatinus, is visited by Sextus, the son of the Roman king, Tarquin. As her husband is away in battle, she provides Sextus with all the hospitality his prestigious rank deserves. During the night, however, he enters her bed chamber and rapes her. Some versions of the story suggest that Sextus gave Lucretia the choice to become his wife and future queen, or being put to death.

In response to the rape, Lucretia dresses in the black colours of mourning and summons her husband and father, asking them to each bring several other witnesses. In one version of the story, Lucretia travels to her father's house in Rome and arranges for her husband to meet her there – but both versions agree that Lucretia tells those gathered what Sextus has done to her, and begs them to vow to avenge her. As they debate what their response should be, Lucretia pulls a knife from beneath her clothing and stabs herself in the heart. She dies in her father's arms. Those gathered all swear upon the bloodied knife to overthrow the tyrannous monarchy that they hold responsible for the crime.

An election is held and the vote is in favour of establishing a republic. Events move quickly, and the monarchy is banished. Collatinus becomes the first consul of Rome, along with Brutus, who had helped organize the revolution.

ABOVE: Relief in limestone representing the she-wolf nursing Romulus and Remus (founders of Rome).

CUPID AND PSYCHE

The story of Cupid and Psyche is told in the only Latin novel to survive in its entirety, *The Golden Ass*, written in the 2nd century CE.

Psyche, the youngest of three daughters, is an alluring mortal whose beauty is such that people neglect to worship Venus, the Roman goddess of love and beauty. This makes Venus extremely jealous and so she hatches a plan to ensure that Psyche will fall in love with a horrible beast. Her son Cupid, the Roman god of erotic love, can make any mortal fall in love by firing one of his golden arrows at them. Venus orders Cupid to fire an arrow at Psyche as she sleeps, so that she will fall in love with the first thing she sees when she wakes. Venus plans to leave a horrible creature in Psyche's bed chamber so that she will forever be in love with it. After a long debate with his mother, Cupid is persuaded to undertake the task, and sets off for Psyche's bed chamber.

THE UNION OF MORTAL AND GOD

However, when Cupid lays eyes on Psyche and sees just how beautiful she really is, he drops the arrow meant for her, and pricks himself with it, immediately falling in love with her. Venus becomes enraged at this, and places a curse on Psyche which means she will never find a husband. In response, a lovesick Cupid refuses to fire any more arrows which would result in no one falling in love ever again and Venus's temple to crumble. His mother finally relents and grants Cupid the right to marry Psyche. Psyche is taken to a far off mountain where her needs are tended by invisible servants during the day. Her new husband visits her only at night, with all lamps extinguished, as he does not want her to know his true identity.

SELF-DEFENCE

Psyche's sisters visit her and persuade her that her husband is a monster who is fattening her up in order to eat her. Afraid of what is in store for her, Psyche decides to save herself from her 'fate' by lighting a lamp one night in order to grab a knife and slay the monster she had married. The lamp lights up the room and instead of a repulsive creature lying next to her she sees a beautiful winged god sleeping quietly next to her. The bright light makes Cupid disappear instantly and Psyche fears, sadly, that she has lost her loved one forever more.

Psyche avenges herself by tricking her sisters into jumping from a mountain top, and then sets out in search of Cupid. She visits Venus and asks her to help, but Venus will only do so on condition that Psyche completes a set of seemingly impossible tasks. First she must separate out all the different types of grain in a large basket before nightfall – a task she manages when an army of ants come to her aid. Next she must retrieve some golden wool from a field full of golden sheep that Venus knows to be vicious and highly dangerous. Acting on the advice of a river god, Psyche waits until noon when the sheep sleep in the shade of the far side of the field, and then is able to safely take the wool. An eagle helps Psyche in her next task, which is to retrieve water from a cleft guarded by serpents.

'TRUE' LOVE

Her final task is to journey to the underworld and return with a piece of the queen of the underworld's beauty in a box. Psyche manages the task, but opens the box, and falls into a permanent sleep. She is rescued by Cupid, who then begs Jupiter, the king of the gods, to help them. Jupiter calls a council of all the gods and explains that it is Cupid's destiny to marry Psyche. The gods agree and issue Psyche with the power of immortality and the two lovers live happily ever after.

Scholars believe that the story of Cupid and Psyche refers to the difference between idealized love and mature love. It is not until the gods believe that mature love, or ever-lasting love, has been reached by the couple that they agree to grant Psyche the power of immortality. The whole time the couple are in the idealized love stage they depict that mortals love the 'idea' of being in love before they reach or find 'true love'. It in turn translates to mean that not all idealized love will turn into mature love.

ABOVE: *Cupid delivering Psyche*, 1871, Sir Edward Burne-Jones (1833-1898).

HERCULES

Although based largely on the Greek myths of Heracles, Hercules has a number of uniquely Roman characteristics and his stories in time grew to somewhat eclipse the originals. It appears the Romans co-opted much of the Greek Heracles and fused his attributes with those of their own mythical shepherd, Garanus, (or Recaranus) in order to create the figure of Hercules, who has captured the imagination of readers ever since. He has taken on a life of his own, stepping out from the shadow of the Greek Heracles to inspire countless artists through the ages, and his image reaches out to us in paintings, statues and engravings across Europe.

A POWERFUL GOD

The Romans believed that Hercules was a god associated with bringing health and vitality, and as the son of the king of all gods, Jupiter, he was considered exceptionally powerful. They erected temples dedicated to him in which they sacrificed animals in order to seek his favour. There were also at least two statues of Hercules at which returning generals would place a percentage of the spoils of war for distribution amongst the citizens of Rome. In Roman mythology he is sometimes pictured with a lyre, as he was also associated with the Muses – the nine

ABOVE: Hercules slaying a dragon while taking the three Golden Apples from the Garden of the Hesperides, circa 1750.

daughters of Zeus who preside over the arts and sciences.

Famously, Hercules was given 12 labours to complete by King Eurystheus as a penance for murdering his own family in a fit of madness (which was induced by his jealous stepmother Juno). The term a 'Herculean feat' has entered the English language as a result of these famous labours.

LION AND SERPENT SLAYER

Hercules's first task is to kill the Nemean Lion and return with its skin. This he manages to do, choosing to wear the lion's skin during his return journey. Eurystheus is so terrified of Hercules's appearance that he hides in a wine jar and sends the details of all future tasks to Hercules via an intermediary.

For his second task, Hercules has to slay the Hydra, a fearsome serpent with nine heads. Discovering that every time he severs one of Hydra's heads she grows two new ones, Hercules calls upon his nephew Iolaus to help him. Iolaus burns each neck stump whenever Hercules severs one of Hydra's heads, and this prevents the heads from growing back.

BOARS, BULLS, AND BIRDS

For his third and fourth tasks, Hercules is required to catch legendary animals and return them to Eurystheus – the Cerynian Hind and Erymanthian Boar. After being successful in both tasks he then has to clean out the vast stables of Augeias in a single day, which he achieves by diverting the course of two rivers so that they flow through the stables. His sixth labour is to rid the land of the fearsome Stymphalian Birds, whose beaks of bronze and metal feathers prove to be no match for Hercules's bow.

Hercules then captures the Cretan Bull with a lasso, before successfully bringing the man-eating Mares of Diomedes to Eurystheus, thus completing his seventh and eighth labours. The ninth labour, set for him by Eurystheus's daughter, is to steal the girdle of Hippolyta, queen of the Amazons. Seduced by Hercules's rippling muscles, Hippolyta surrenders the girdle without a fight.

POISON ARROW

Hercules's tenth labour provides an example of how the Romans embellished the earlier Greek tale of Heracles. Asked to obtain the cattle of the giant Geryon, Hercules kills Geryon with an arrow that has been dipped in the poison of the Hydra. In the Greek version Heracles then returns with Geryon's cattle – but the Roman Hercules must overcome a further obstacle in the form of the fire-breathing half-human monster Cacus (son of Vulcan) who steals the cattle from Hercules and hides them in a cave. Hercules strangles Cacus so tightly that his eyes pop out. By killing Cacus, Hercules frees the local population from the monster's tyranny and is lauded throughout the land.

After stealing the apples from the blissful garden of the nymphs Hesperides (with the help of the mighty titan Atlas), Hercules finally completes his labours by capturing Cerberus, the three-headed dog that guards the gates to Hades. Eurystheus agrees to release Hercules from further labours if he will return the fearsome hound back to the underworld.

VULCAN

Another good example of how the Romans assimilated the myths of other cultures, the story of Vulcan is borrowed from the Greek myths surrounding Hephaestus. In the Roman version, Vulcan lives beneath Mount Etna, and it is from Vulcan that the modern English word 'Volcano' derives. The Romans built bonfires to placate him at their Volcania festival that was held on August 23 each year.

SAVED BY A SEA NYMPH

Vulcan is the son of Jupiter, the king of the gods, and his wife Juno, queen of the gods. On the birth of her son, Juno finds Vulcan to be so ugly that she throws him, in disgust, from the top of Mount Olympus. In his fall into the sea, Vulcan breaks his leg, which was never to fully heal but he survives and is taken in by the sea nymph Thetis in her underwater kingdom, where she raises him as her own son. Vulcan's childhood turns into an extremely happy one spending time with sea creatures and playing on the beach, which results in him finding a fisherman's fire on the beach. Vulcan becomes engrossed with the dancing flame of the fire and places it in a clam shell and takes it back into the sea, where he uses it to become a blacksmith making beautiful objects out of the precious metals he discovers the fire can make.

ERUPTIONS

Vulcan's mother learns of her son's survival after Thetis attends a party on Mount Olympus wearing a beautiful necklace that Vulcan has made for her. Juno insists that Vulcan return home, but he refuses and instead sends her a gift which is a beautifully embellished throne of gold. When Juno sits on the throne, however, metal bands spring shut and trap her. She is unable to move for three days, and no one can free her.

Jupiter tells Vulcan that if he will release Juno from the trap he will allow Vulcan to marry Venus, the Roman goddess of love and beauty. Vulcan agrees and the two are married. Vulcan continues with his beautiful works and builds himself a smithery under Mount Etna. Whenever Venus is unfaithful, Vulcan angrily sends sparks from Mount Etna which appear in the form of volcanic eruptions.

RIGHT: Copper plate etching showing Roman god Vulcan at work at an anvil. From *The War. Habits of the Romans*, 1824.

THE CELTS & THE BRITISH

Even though much of Europe was once ruled by the Celts, many of the gods they worshipped and the stories they told have been lost. The Celts were not primarily a literate society, and so we have to rely on Roman historians, and later the monks of the Middle Ages, for many of our records of Celtic mythology. There may have been a considerable tension between the desire of the monks to record the myths of their native cultures, and their hostility towards many of the pagan beliefs that the myths underpinned, so many stories may have changed enormously from their original plot and meaning.

The various tribes that we collectively call the Celts almost certainly each had their own individual myths, but common themes and storylines run between them which hint at certain shared beliefs.

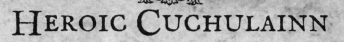

HEROIC CUCHULAINN

The Ulster Cycle features one of the greatest of all Celtic heroes, Cuchulainn, the son of the god Lugh. Cuchulainn was a character of legendary strength and bravery, originally named Setanta, who was given the name Cuchulainn at the age of six after killing the guard dog of a blacksmith, called Culann, with his bare hands.

A whole series of battles and tests of strength are outlined in the Ulster Cycle, and Cuchulainn invariably emerges triumphant. In one famous tale, Conall, Laoghaire, and Cuchulainn are tested by a giant who allows them each to chop his head off as long as he can then chop off theirs. Conall and Laoghaire both cut off the giant's head but run away when he places it back on his neck. Cuchulainn, having also chopped the giant's head off, bows his neck and allows the giant to cut off his head. The giant, who transpires to be a magician, pronounces Cuchulainn the bravest man in Ulster, and disappears.

AN EPIC BATTLE

Cuchulainn eventually dies at the hands of the forces of Connaught in a monumental battle known as Tain Bo Cuailnge (The Cattle Raid Of Cooley). After being struck with a spear, he ties himself to a post so that he might continue to face his enemies standing, and as his sword falls from his hand, it cuts off the hand of his killer.

FINN MACCOOL

The Fenian Cycle chiefly concerns the deeds of Finn MacCool (Fionn Mac Cumhall) in the 3rd century. The tales are romantic in style and written largely in verse. Finn MacCool was the son of a chieftain from the warrior band known as the Fianna, who died in battle just as his wife gave birth to him.

POWERFUL WARRIORS

His mother, fearing that she would lose her son as she had her husband, took Finn into hiding where she brought him up with the help of two warrior women. The warriors taught Finn the skills of fighting and he grew into a strong man.

His mother and the female warriors knew he now had the strength but needed to go into the world alone in order to gather the necessary wisdom to take over his dead father's role of chieftain. Finn searches for the poet and wise man, Finegas, to help him with this task.

SALMON OF KNOWLEDGE

Finn found Finegas beside a lake, where he had spent the last seven years trying to catch the Salmon of Knowledge – a magical fish that would give the person that ate it the power to see into the past and the future. Having burned his thumb whilst cooking the powerful fish for Finegas, Finn sucked on it in order to ease the pain and thus accidentally tasted the salmon. At that moment all the powers of the Salmon flowed into Finn. The wise man knew then that it was Finn's destiny and not his own to gain the fish's wisdom and Finn went on to be a hero, undertaking numerous battles and adventures as chief of the Fiannas.

BANSHEES

The word banshee comes from the Irish *bean sidhe* meaning 'woman of the side' or 'woman of the fairy mound'. These female spirits are believed to be sent from the underworld as omens of death. Although usually thought of as ugly old hags, banshees can take many forms, including that of a beautiful young seductive woman, as well as a host of animal forms (most usually a crow or a hare). Banshees are also associated with washer women, and are sometimes seen washing the blood from clothes or armour.

BEWARE OF HAIR

Said to have long fair hair which they brush with a silver comb, banshees dress in cloaks of grey (or on occasion red, green or black). It is said that if you find a comb on the ground in Ireland you should never pick it up, as it may have been left by a banshee attempting to entrap you.

WAILING BANSHEE

Perhaps more terrifying than the sight of a banshee is the sound of one – the howl of the banshee is legendary in its spine-chilling mournfulness. They are reported to be most commonly heard during the night, and in the proximity of woods and forests. Whilst usually screeching in tone, in some parts of Ireland the banshee's song is described as having a beautiful lilting sound, though it is still perceived to be a lament. Banshees also appear in Scottish legends, and the Welsh Gwrach-y-Rhibyn or Hag Of The Mist is a similar spirit whose cry also foretells a coming death.

THE STONE OF SCONE

Used for centuries as the coronation stone for Scottish royalty, The Stone of Scone (or Stone of Destiny) was said to have been used as a pillow by Jacob in biblical times. The first king to have been seated on the stone was Kenneth MacAlpin around 847 CE, king of the Picts and believed by many to be the first true king of Scotland.

The last Scottish king to be crowned upon the stone was John Balliol in 1292, before the stone was captured by King Edward I of England in 1296 and transported to Westminster Abbey in London. There it remained under the English coronation throne for 700 years until finally being handed back in 1996. It is now housed in Edinburgh Castle, though it will be returned to Westminster Abbey when required for future coronations of British royalty.

An oblong block of red sandstone, the stone is closely associated with the Irish Blarney Stone and *Lia Fail* – the stone used at the coronations of the ancient High Kings of Ireland. The stone is steeped in legend as well as history: it is said to roar when the rightful king places his feet upon it, and has the power to rejuvenate those of royal blood.

THE BLARNEY STONE

A block of bluestone built into the battlements of Blarney Castle around five miles from Cork in the south of Ireland, The Blarney Stone is said to give anyone who kisses it 'the gift of the gab' (the ability to flatter and seduce with words). Said to have been given to Cormac McCarthy by Robert the Bruce in 1314 as a token of thanks for McCarthy's role in the Battle of Bannockburn, it is believed that the stone was set into the castle in 1446.

A Shroud of Mystery

There are many theories as to where the stone originally came from, including legends that state it was part of the wailing wall in Jerusalem, or half of the original Stone of Scone (the stone sat on by the monarchs of Scotland during their coronation services, see opposite page).

The stone is now a major tourist attraction in Ireland. Kissing the stone involves leaning backwards over the edge of a parapet – an action recently made considerably easier thanks to the installation of guard rails. In earlier times a person would have to be held by the ankles and dangled over the side of the castle. Whilst the stone itself is undoubtedly of great antiquity, the legend associated with it appears to date from relatively recent times, probably the late 18th century.

ABOVE: A girl lies flat on the ground, in order to kiss the Blarney Stone in Blarney Castle, Cork city.

THE LOCH NESS MONSTER

The legend that a dinosaur-like monster lurks beneath the depths of Loch Ness in the Scottish Highlands has become world-famous since it came to the attention of the media in the 1930s. Affectionately known as 'Nessie', the creature has been the subject of extensive searches but if it does exist it has yet to be caught, or even photographed clearly.

SURGEON'S MONSTER

The *Inverness Courier* carried the first modern era report of a sighting of the monster in 1933 by English holidaymaker George Spicer. The paper then received a flood of letters from others claiming to have also seen the creature, described as having an elongated neck like the plesiosaurs of the dinosaur age. The legend truly took off in the popular imagination after photographs were published of what purported to be the monster in 1933 and 1934. The most famous of these, the so-called 'Surgeon's Photograph' (as it was taken by gynaecologist Robert Kenneth Wilson, who at the time wished to remain anonymous), was revealed to be a hoax in 1994. The hoaxers fixed the sculpted head of a sea creature on to a toy submarine in order to fool *The Daily Mail* (the newspaper that first published the photograph).

WATER BEAST

Believers in Nessie point to a 7th century account of a 'water beast' in the River Ness as proof of a long association between the loch and sea monsters. Sceptics, however, suggest that accounts of water beasts were common during this period, that the creature is said to be in the river rather than the loch, and that the creature in question may have been of zoological rather than crypto-zoological origin.

The most recent and comprehensive in a long series of surveys was carried out on behalf of the BBC in 2003, using sonar

ABOVE: A view of the Loch Ness Monster, near Inverness, Scotland, April 19, 1934. The photograph, one of two pictures known as the 'surgeon's photographs,' was allegedly taken by Colonel Robert Kenneth Wilson, though it was later exposed as a hoax.

beams and satellite tracking. It found no evidence of any large creatures living in the loch. A variety of rational explanations have been offered to explain the rash of sightings of the monster, including optical illusions, misidentification of water-dwelling animals and even the suggestion that the first sightings may have been of an elephant from a travelling circus.

NESSIE SPOTTING

Thousands of tourists flock to Loch Ness every year in the hopes of glimpsing the monster for themselves, and sceptics have suggested that the lucrative tourist trade is one of the main drivers for the legend continuing to be propagated.

THE MABINOGION

The stories of the Mabinogion were originally written down in Welsh in the 14th century, but their roots lie at least two centuries earlier and many believe they are more ancient still. The eleven prose stories were described in *The White Book of Rydderch* and *The Red Book Of Hergest* and are organized into four Branches of The Mabinogi (which represent The Mabinogion proper), plus four Native Tales, and three Romances. Within the stories lie what are believed by many to be the earliest references to the Arthurian legend.

RHIANNON AND PWYLL

Rhiannon is an important influence throughout the Mabinogion, particularly in the third branch, but also in the first branch, which tells the story of her marriage to the hero Pwyll, King of Dyfed.

Having swapped places with the king of the underworld (Arawn) for a year and defeated the king's enemy Hafgan, Pwyll is returning home when he spots a beautiful maiden dressed in gold and riding a mysterious white horse. He sends his horsemen to stop her, but they can never manage to catch up with her, even though she appears to canter at a leisurely pace. At last Pwyll himself tries to catch the maiden, and manages to draw alongside her simply by asking her to stop. The two fall in love at first sight.

MAGIC BAG

She tells Pwyll her name is Rhiannon, and that she is betrothed to a man called Gwawl, but would rather marry Pwyll. Rhiannon gives Pwyll a magic bag that can never be fully filled and advises him on how to trick Gwawl to climb inside it. Pwyll follows her instructions and he and his men beat Gwawl once he is captured in the bag, until he agrees to release Rhiannon from her betrothal in return for being released from the bag. Pwyll and Rhiannon marry, and shortly afterwards give birth to a son, Pryderi (see the following page).

Rhiannon may be associated with the earlier Celtic goddess Epona, who is discussed later on in this chapter. Epona was widely worshipped through the prehistoric Celtic world as a horse goddess, and was depicted as an ethereal maiden on horseback in much the same way as Rhiannon is in the first branch of The Mabinogion.

PRYDERI

The character of Pryderi features in all four branches of the Mabinogion, though he is a relatively minor character in the second branch.

Shortly after his birth, Pryderi disappears while in the care of his mother's ladies-in-waiting. Fearing they will be in trouble, the ladies-in-waiting smear blood on the mouth of his mother Rhiannon, and claim that she ate her own son during the night. Rhiannon is punished by being forced to carry visitors to the court on her back.

Pryderi is discovered in a stable by Teyrnon, Lord of Gwent, who rescues him from a mysterious beast before adopting him and naming him Gwri. A few years later, Teyrnon realizes the true identity of his charge and returns him to Rhiannon and Pwyll, who rename him Pryderi.

THE GOLDEN BOWL

Pryderi marries Cigfa and becomes King of Dyfed when his father dies. His mother remarries with Manawydan, who fought with Pryderi in Ireland and was one of only seven Welshmen to return alive. While out hunting, Pryderi follows a white boar which leads him to a magical tower, within which lies a golden bowl. As soon as Pryderi touches the bowl he finds he cannot move or speak. His mother Rhiannon follows him to the tower and becomes enchanted by the same spell, at which point the tower disappears.

PLAGUE OF MICE

Cigfa and Manawydan farm some land together, but are plagued with mice until Manawydan captures one particularly fat mouse and decides to hang it. The magician Llwyd ap Cil Coed intervenes, revealing that the mouse is his pregnant wife. He tells Cigfa and Manawydan that he cast the spell on Pryderi and Rhiannon to avenge Gwawl, whose advances Rhiannon had rejected in order to marry Pwyll. He offers to lift the spell if Manawydan will spare his wife. Manawydan agrees to the proposal and Pryderi and Rhiannon reappear.

Pryderi later has his herd of pigs stolen by another magician, Gwydion, who tricks him into swapping them for a herd of horses which turns out to be an illusion. Pryderi wages war against Gwydion, until the two agree to settle their differences in single combat. On the appointed day of battle, Pryderi is killed by Gwydion.

MERLIN

The figure of Merlin was popularized by Geoffrey of Monmouth in the 12th century, but has been embellished upon by countless other writers since. Merlin appears to have evolved from the early Welsh legend of Myrddin Wyllt, who was a bard driven mad by the horrors of war in the 6th century. Myrddin went to live amongst the beasts of the forests, where he developed the gift of prophesy. The most famous of his prophesies came true when he died a 'triple death' of falling, stabbing and drowning – he was chased off a cliff, and impaled himself on a spike with his head beneath the water.

Geoffrey of Monmouth also drew upon a 9th century manuscript, *The Historia Brittonum* (or History of the Britains) to place Merlin at the centre of a story about King Vortigern, who invited the Saxons to settle in the British Isles. Vortigern tries repeatedly to build a stronghold near Mount Snowdon in North Wales, but each time he is thwarted (the building either falls down, or the materials are stolen, depending on which version of the story you hold to). Vortigern is advised to sprinkle the blood of a boy born without a father on the ground to ensure that his building project is successful.

TWO DRAGONS

The boy in question is Merlin, though he also uses the name of Aurelius Ambrosius in Geoffrey's tale. Merlin reveals to Vortigern the real reason for his problems: a red dragon and a white dragon are fighting one another beneath the ground, and disturbing the earth that Vortigern is trying to build on. The two dragons had been imprisoned beneath the ground by King Lludd in one of the tales of The Mabinogion.

Vortigern digs open the ground and frees the two dragons, which continue to fight until the red dragon finally defeats the white dragon.

Merlin tells Vortigern that the white dragon symbolizes the Saxon people, and the red dragon symbolizes the native British people. The victory of the red dragon is a prophesy of the coming of King Arthur, whose father's name was Uther Pendragon – or 'chief dragon'.

MERLIN'S POWERS

In later stories, Merlin becomes the tutor of the young King Arthur and is responsible for building the magic sword Excalibur and the round table that Arthur's knights meet at. He falls in love with the beautiful young girl Nimue, who persuades him to teach her his spells. Nimue betrays Merlin and traps him forever, either in a cave or in an enchanted wood. Merlin has prophesized all of this, and is powerless to prevent it.

In some versions of the story Nimue is a tragic figure who only betrays Merlin because she is prophesized to do so, and once the prophesy is complete she kills herself. In yet other versions she is the fabled Lady of the Lake, who receives the sword Excalibur after Arthur's death.

ABOVE: Ms Fr. 95 f.268 Merlin dictates the story to Blaise – French School, from *L'Histoire de Merlin* by Robert de Boron, circa 1280-90.

KING ARTHUR AND THE KNIGHTS OF THE ROUND TABLE

Arthur was the illegitimate son of Uther Pendragon and Igraine, the queen of Tintagel. The queen was married to Gorlois, and Uther gained access to her after Merlin cast a spell allowing him to take Gorlois's form. In most versions of the story Arthur is raised by Merlin, and proves his right to succeed Uther Pendragon by pulling a sword from a stone at the age of 15. Some accounts say that this sword was the magic sword Excalibur, but others have it that Arthur came into possession of Excalibur after rowing out onto a lake and taking the sword from The Lady of the Lake, whose hand emerged from beneath the water, clasping Excalibur. The scabbard of the sword is said to prevent Arthur from losing blood when hurt in combat, and he later fights many successful battles against the Saxons, Scots and Picts, in addition to defeating the Romans.

ABOVE: *Sir Galahad is Welcomed to the Round Table,* anon, circa 1380-85.

GUINEVERE

Arthur establishes a base at the magical castle of Camelot, where he gathers the most brilliant knights of the kingdom at a round table. He falls in love with and marries the princess Guinevere. In the most commonly retold version of the legend, Guinevere is secretly in love with Lancelot, one of Arthur's Knights of the Round Table. Arthur's son Mordred learns of the affair between Guinevere and Lancelot, and tells his father, whom he hopes to dethrone. Arthur condemns his wife to death, but she is rescued by Lancelot, and the two escape to Lancelot's castle (Joyous Gard, thought to be in the North of England). A bloody battle ensues between Arthur and Lancelot, but it is cut short when Arthur's son Mordred attempts to usurp his father as King of Britain.

POWER STRUGGLE

In some versions of the story, it is Mordred who has an affair with Guinevere, his own mother. What the accounts seem to agree on is that at some stage while Arthur is away at battle, Mordred seizes the throne. Arthur returns and after a fierce struggle kills his son in one-to-one combat. Arthur is himself mortally wounded, however, and is taken to a lake by Sir Bedivere (another of the Knights of the Round Table). Bedivere throws Excalibur back into the lake, where it is received by the hand of The Lady of the Lake. Arthur then sails off in a boat across the lake to the magical kingdom of Avalon. Lancelot, who has ridden to Arthur's aid, arrives too late, and retires to Glastonbury to pray for forgiveness.

It is said that Arthur is merely sleeping, and will return when Britain most needs him. He maintains his youth by drinking from the Holy Grail.

THE HOLY GRAIL

Said to be the cup (or plate) from which Christ drank at The Last Supper, and which Joseph used to collect his blood at the crucifixion, the grail is believed to hold the secret to eternal life.

In all major versions of the legend, Joseph brings the Holy Grail to Britain, where its keeper is the Fisher King, a ruler badly maimed in the thigh or genitals, often by a magical weapon. The Fisher King can only be healed by a knight with a pure heart, and until the chosen knight arrives the kingdom remains a wasteland whilst the King is reduced to fishing beside his castle. In the original story of *The Quest For The Holy Grail*, Percival is the only Knight of the Round Table who possesses the qualities to heal the Fisher King and thus gain access to the Holy Grail. In a later version Galahad, the son of Lancelot, is the chosen knight. Galahad takes the Holy Grail back to the Holy Land, and it disappears after he dies.

The myth of the grail may have evolved from earlier Celtic myths about magical objects which could restore life or perform other miracles. A cauldron which can bring the dead back to life is mentioned in the tale of Bran The Blessed, a giant who appears in the second branch of the Welsh Mabinogion. The fabled 'Thirteen Treasures of the Island of Britain', mentioned in Welsh texts from the 15th and 16th centuries, includes objects which can provide everlasting amounts of food and can distinguish between the brave and the cowardly.

THE LEGEND OF ROBIN HOOD

Most commonly associated with Sherwood Forest in the English midlands, Robin Hood and his band are famous for robbing from the rich and giving the proceeds to the poor. Since the first stories, dating from the 15th century, many additions have been made to the legend, including the 'Merry Men' title for his fellow outlaws. The most important of the Merry Men are Little John, Will Scarlet, Friar Tuck and Much the Miller's Son. Other notable figures in the stories are The Sheriff of Nottingham, Robin's arch enemy, and Maid Marian, Robin's female companion.

FIGHTING FOR JUSTICE

The stories themselves contain no specific examples of Robin 'giving to the poor', focussing more regularly on him stealing from the rich, and evading capture by the Sheriff of Nottingham. Robin is usually presented as a skilled swordsman, and later as a superb archer who is rarely without his trusty bow and arrow. Impetuous and violent in the early tales, he becomes more gentlemanly in later stories, which often have a comedic element. Although he was a 'commoner' in the original stories, he gradually evolved into an aristocratic character whose land had been wrongfully confiscated from him.

It is believed that the name 'Robin Hood' derives from a shorthand term dating back to the 11th century which was used for any outlaw or fugitive. Many real life characters have been suggested as candidates for the real Robin Hood but it is more likely that he was based on an amalgamation of different characters.

ABOVE: *Robin Hood and his Merry Men Entertaining Richard the Lionheart in Sherwood Forest*, Daniel Maclise (1806-1870).

SAINT GEORGE AND THE DRAGON

The English myth of Saint George and the dragon is believed to have originated as a medieval reworking of the Greek myth of Perseus and Andromeda, though others have cited links with even earlier stories told by the Phrygians and Thracians. The central action of the story, in which a hero slays a dragon or serpent, seems to be as old as stories themselves and appears in the myths of almost every culture. After the advent of Christianity, dragons became closely associated with the devil.

In England, the version in which Saint George is the hero became popular in the Middle Ages after being included in Jacobus de Voragine's *Golden Legend*, a collection of myths about saints. Many other versions of the legend exist, however, and the location and details of the story change according to the storyteller. The bare bones of the story in each case are similar: a town is terrorized by a dragon, a king offers the dragon a young princess to appease it, and Saint George rides to the town in order to slay the dragon and rescue the princess.

Jacobus de Voragine sets the action in modern-day Libya. In this version the people of the town begin by feeding the dragon a sheep each day, but then resort to feeding it their own children, who are chosen by lottery. When the lottery falls upon the king's daughter, the king offers the people half of all his riches if his daughter can be spared. The people refuse and the princess, dressed in silk (or as a bride in some versions), is sent to the lake where the dragon dwells. In many versions the dragon lives in a cave, and the princess is the last maiden left in the town not already fed to the dragon.

A CHRISTIAN MISSIONARY

Saint George rides past by chance, and insists on helping the princess. When the dragon appears, George is sure to make the Christian 'sign of the cross' before charging the dragon and badly injuring it with his lance (Ascalon, in some versions a sword rather than a lance). He then calls upon the princess to throw him her girdle, which he wraps around the dragon's head to use as a collar. Tamed, the fearsome dragon is led back to the town where George tells the people of the power of God. They convert to Christianity and George slays the dragon.

Some versions tell that George first attempts to use his lance on the dragon, but it shatters against the dragon's hard scales. George then rolls under a magical orange tree which protects him from the dragon, allowing him to regain his strength. Battle is joined for a second time, and the dragon breathes fire or poison upon George, destroying his armour. He again rolls under the magical orange tree to escape. When he recovers, he attacks the dragon for a third and final time, this time using his sword to pierce the dragon at its only vulnerable spot, beneath its wing.

Saint George's heraldic shield of a red cross on a white background was adopted by the English during the Crusades, and he was adopted as the official patron saint of England in the 14th century.

RIGHT: *St George Slaying the Dragon*, Emmanuel Tzanes (1637–1694).

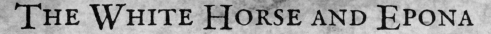

THE WHITE HORSE AND EPONA

The White Horse is a stylized prehistoric hill figure cut into the white chalk of White Horse Hill in Uffington, England. It has been described as a horse since at least the 11th century, though some commentators believe it is really a dragon. At 374 feet long it is clearly visible from the nearby Uffington Castle, which dates from the Iron Age, and may have been created by the builders of the castle. Archaeological excavations have revealed it to be at least 3,000 years old, making it the oldest hill figure in Britain.

IRON AGE DEITY

The figure may represent a horse goddess connected with a local tribe – many experts suggest it may be Epona, who was one of the few goddesses widely worshipped across Iron Age Europe and was also adopted as a deity by the Romans. Epona is a protector of horses, and also has associations with fertility, often being depicted holding ears of grain. For the Romans, she evolved into a protector of cavalry, and images of her have been found in barns and stables across the ancient Roman empire.

She may have been the inspiration for Rhiannon, the mysterious horse-riding maiden of The Mabinogion, and for the legend of Lady Godiva who is said to have ridden naked through the streets of Coventry in protest at the high taxes that her husband, Leofric the Earl of Mercia, was imposing on his tenants. Epona was frequently depicted as riding naked or half-naked, with her long hair covering her body.

HORSE OR DRAGON?

Epona is not believed to have been worshipped until 1,000 years after the White Horse was created, and thus it seems she either evolved from an earlier goddess or the horse does not represent her at all. One widely circulated legend states that the horse was commissioned by King Alfred to commemorate his victory over the Danes – however this event did not occur until 871. A second legend states that the horse is in fact a dragon, and it symbolizes the dragon that Saint George famously killed.

BEOWULF

An epic poem of over 3,000 lines, written in Old English sometime before the 11th century. It is the story of a heroic warrior, Beowulf, and his battles in Denmark and Sweden. Firstly Beowulf kills the monster Grendel, who has been attacking the subjects of King Hroogar of Denmark. He fights Grendel unarmed, so as not to be at any sort of advantage over him, and kills him by pulling off one of the monster's arms.

Next Beowulf fights Grendel's mother in her lair at the bottom of a lake. He first uses a magical sword called Hrunting, but Grendel's mother is immune to its power and so Beowulf slays her with a sword from her own armoury, which was crafted by giants.

THE DRAGON'S TREASURE

Beowulf becomes king, and later in his reign he battles a dragon, which has become enraged by the theft of the treasure it was hoarding. Beowulf prevails against the dragon, with the help of Wiglaf, the only one of his warriors brave enough to stand by his side. However, Beowulf is mortally injured in the fight, and after his death is buried beside the sea with the dragon's treasure, which is said to be cursed.

LEGENDARY LOST ISLANDS OF BRITAIN

There are several legends of lost islands off the coast of Britain, which have clear parallels with the legend of Atlantis outlined by Plato. The Welsh believed in the lost land of Cantre'r Gwaelod which was said to have once existed in Cardigan Bay. Church bells are said to be heard ringing out from the lost kingdom in times of danger. The remains of a prehistoric sunken forest at nearby Borth suggest that there may well have been communities living in lands lost to the seas, and the myth may have evolved from this historical fact.

The Celtic brethren of the Welsh in Cornwall have the legend of Lyonnesse, which was said to have once connected Cornwall (in southern England) with the Scilly Isles. Lyonnesse was mentioned as the home of the hero Tristan's father in later Arthurian legends. Lord Tennyson's epic poem *Idylls of the King* describes Lyonnesse as the site of the final battle between King Arthur and his sworn enemy, his son Mordred.

Lyonnesse seems closely associated with the Breton myth of Ys, a city built on the coast of Brittany and swallowed by the ocean after the devil tricked the king of Ys into handing him the key to the dyke that protected Ys. As with Cantre'r Gwaelod, it is said the church bells can still be heard ringing from time to time. The legend also states that when the French capital city Paris is drowned under water then Ys will rise again.

ABOVE: The elderly Beowulf finally dies after an encounter with a dragon.

OTHER EUROPEAN MYTHOLOGY

All European cultures have their own sets of myths and legends, some which overlap with other societies and some that are specific to the people of that land. From the epic Norse sagas, *Prose Edda* and *Poetic Edda* to the Green Man of Western Europe and Olentzero of the Basque Country these ancient stories have been passed down through generations and have stood the test of time.

NORSE CREATION MYTH

In the Norse creation myth, the Earth is created from the body of Ymir, a giant who came into being when a world of ice was melted by a world of fire. Ymir is suckled by the primordial cow Audumla, who licks at salty ice blocks in order to feed herself. As she licks, the form of a man is revealed – Buri, who in turn fathers Borr. Ymir is slain by Borr's three sons, Odin, Vili and Ve, who use Ymir's body parts to fashion the earth, seas and sky, and then create men from driftwood. In total the sons create nine worlds, with Midgard (or middle land) serving as a home for the first humans, Askr and Embla. They also construct a formidable citadel called Asgard, to protect themselves from the ice giants.

THE CHILDREN OF NJÖRD

As well as the Aesir gods of Asgard, there was another family of gods in Norse mythology called the Vanir who lived in the separate world of Vanaheimr. It is said that at first the two types of gods were at war with one another, but in time they made peace and combined forces to do battle with the giants. Perhaps the most important of the Vanir in terms of the myths are Freyr and Freyja, the children of the sea god Njörd. They both have voracious sexual appetites, and are associated with fertility and birth in Norse mythology. The desire of the giants to capture Freyja is a major cause of friction between the gods and the giants in the stories.

ODIN

Odin was the most important of the Norse gods, and became known as Woden in Anglo-Saxon mythology. He may also have parallels with the Celtic God Lugus – both are associated with a spear (Gungnir, a magic spear which never misses its target, in Odin's case) and ravens. In Odin's case his two ravens fly around the Earth each day and inform him of all the main happenings in the world each night. Often depicted riding his eight-legged horse, Sleipnir, Odin is a complex god, associated with war and death but also poetry and magic. In total he is referred to by over 200 different names in various Norse sagas, including Yggr (terror), Alfodr (Father of All) and, most significantly in terms of his legacy, Sigfodr (Father of Victory). Interestingly, Wednesday is named after him and he is seen as the equivalent of the Greek god Mercury in this respect.

VOLVA

In the first poem of the *Poetic Edda* (Voluspa), Odin is told the story of his past (the creation myth) and also much of his future by a Volva – a female fortune teller common in Norse myth. The Volva tells him, amongst other things, that he will sacrifice an eye at Mimir's Well in order to drink from the well and gain wisdom, and that he will ultimately be killed by the great wolf Fenrir.

Odin's journey to Mimir's Well in the land of the giants is described in the Icelandic *Ynglinga Saga*, and as the prophesy had suggested he does indeed sacrifice an eye in order to gain wisdom. It is said that he saw all of the sorrows that would come to fall upon humanity and the gods. His eye is said to remain at the bottom of the well as a symbol of the price of knowledge.

ABOVE: Odin (Wotan), god of wisdom and war, sitting on throne, engraving, 1883.

SECRET OF THE RUNES

A second story tells that Odin obtained supernatural wisdom and discovered the secrets of the runes by hanging from Yggdrasil, the world tree (see the following page), for nine days and nine nights whilst pierced in the side with his own spear. The medieval German chronicler Adam of Bremen attested that every ninth year people from all over Sweden gathered at a temple in Uppsala and hung slaves from trees as sacrifices to Odin.

The belief that Odin could bring victory in war persisted in Scandinavia for many centuries, with the last battle credited to his divine influence taking place in 1208, when Eric X of Sweden fought the former king Sverker at the Battle of Lena. Eric was heavily outnumbered, but according to legend Odin appeared at the front of the Swedish forces (riding the eight-legged horse Sleipnir) and led them to a famous victory.

THOR

hor, the red-haired and red-bearded god of thunder, and the son of Odin, was one of the most popular Norse deities. Revered by ancient pre-Christian Germanic tribes, his influence lasted long into the Viking era. He wielded a giant hammer called Mjollnir, which always returned to his hand after he had thrown it. To lift the mighty hammer Thor needed a magical belt which increased his strength, and a pair of iron gloves.

The Anglo-Saxon word thunder was named after him as was Thursday. The day was considered so important that even after their Christianization many people from Flanders were still treating Thursday as a holy day as late as the 7th century.

THUNDER CLAPS

The sound of thunder was believed to come from the pots and pans that he hung from his chariot, which was pulled by a pair of winged goats called Tanngrisnir and Tanngnjostr – it is believed that Thor kills the goats for meat at the end of each day before resurrecting them again with his magical hammer.

In one famous story from the *Prose Edda*, a king of the giants called Thrym steals Thor's hammer, and refuses to return it unless he is given the fertility goddess Freyja as a bride. With the help of the cunning Loki (see page 56), Thor hatches a plan to steal back his hammer by disguising himself as Freyja. Dressed as a bride in one of Freyja's gowns and a veil, Thor rides to Thrym's wedding feast. The king is stunned to witness the great thirst and appetite of his bride at the feast, but Loki explains that she has not eaten for many days due to her excitement at the forthcoming wedding. When Thrym places Thor's hammer in the lap of his bride to bless her, Thor tears off his disguise and uses the hammer to kill all of the giants in the room.

Thor is said to live with his wife Sif and their children in the finest hall in Valhalla (discussed on page 58), the hall containing some 540 rooms.

LOKI

Loki is described as a god by some sources and as a giant (or jötunn) by others, and his relationship to the gods also seems to vary depending on the teller of the story. He sometimes helps the other gods, and sometimes causes problems for them. In his role either as helper or mischief-maker, he features in many of the most important Norse myths.

In the poem *Lokasenna*, Loki is chased away from a feast after killing a servant, but re-enters the hall to argue with and insult all of the other gods gathered there (perhaps under the influence of mead). Thor arrives at the feast and is in no mood for Loki's insults, and Loki recognizes that it is time to beat a hasty retreat. Despite turning himself into a salmon and hiding in a waterfall, he

is caught by the angry gods and tied up with the entrails of his own son. A serpent fastened above Loki drips venom over his face, and the ground shakes as he writhes in agonizing pain (which was believed to be the explanation for earthquakes). The venom is collected in a bowl by his wife and emptied when the bowl becomes full.

The ambivalent, fractious relationship between Loki and the gods of Asgard ultimately ends in bloody conflict after he tricks the blind god Hoor into killing the god Baldr with a spear. This incident is one of the major triggers for the final battle of Ragnarök (see page 58). Loki fights on the side of the giants against the god Heimdallr and both die as a result of the encounter.

YGGDRASIL – THE WORLD TREE

The 'world tree' Yggdrasil was a giant ash tree, central to Norse belief. The nine worlds of the universe exist around it, and the gods gather at Yggdrasil daily to hold their courts. The exact relationship between the nine worlds and Yggdrasil is never explicitly stated, and the location and nature of the worlds may have changed over time. However, it is said that the branches of Yggdrasil stretch high into the heavens, and beneath its three roots lie the realm of Hel (an underworld presided over by a being of the same name), the realm of the frost giants and the realm of mankind. Yggdrasil is often depicted with

an eagle in its branches and a snake coiled around its roots. The name of the tree is believed to derive from *Ygg drasill* which translates as Odin's horse, though some have suggested that it derives from the old Norse word *Yggr* meaning terror.

It is not made clear what happens to Yggdrasil after the ultimate battle of Ragnarök (see page 58) but the tree was said to shake as a portent of the coming disaster.

The worship of holy trees was common throughout prehistoric Europe and is also found in the ancient mythologies of Asia.

RIGHT: Yggdrasil – the sacred ash – the Mundane Tree of Norse mythology whose branches overhang the Universe.

Valhalla and Ragnarök

Valhalla (hall of the heroes or hall of the slain) is a heavenly hall in Asgard, where the bravest Norse warriors go after their deaths, to be welcomed by Odin as they wait for the final battle, Ragnarök. Its roof is made from overlapping shields, held up by the shafts of spears. Directly outside the front door of Valhalla stands Glasir, a tree with golden leaves.

The dead warriors are transported to Valhalla by female warriors wearing swan feathers, The Valkyries. There they are served an endless supply of mead and wild boar, though Odin himself only ever drinks the mead, feeding the boar to his two wolves, Geri and Freki. The inhabitants of Valhalla pass their time practising hand-to-hand combat with one another, playing games of chance and performing juggling tricks with swords.

WARRIORS ARRIVAL

Fallen warriors were believed to arrive at Valhalla carrying whatever possessions had been placed on their funeral pyre or buried in the ground for them. Odin outlines the procedure for Norse funerals in the *Ynglinga saga* (written by the Icelandic poet Snorri Sturluson), stating that cremation ashes should either be buried or taken out to sea and scattered.

One of the most striking images to survive from ancient Norse culture, the Tjangvide image stone, appears to show a valkyrie welcoming a deceased warrior to Valhalla. Found in 1844 the stone is believed to date from the 8th century, and is now one of the most prized exhibits at the Swedish Museum Of National Antiquities in Stockholm. The dead man appears to have crossed to Valhalla in a longship, depicted in the bottom half of the image. Some interpret the image as a valkyrie offering a horn filled with wine to Odin.

Ragnarök is the epic battle between good and evil which finally claims the lives of the major Norse Gods. The battle itself has been prophesied and is foreshadowed by a series of natural disasters and portents of destruction. Odin and the warriors from Valhalla clash with Loki and the giants from the world of Jotunheimr (separated from the human world by mountains and forests). In the course of the battle Odin dies whilst doing battle with the mighty wolf Fenrir, before his son Vidar breaks Fenrir's mighty jaws with his bare hands. The god Freyr is killed by a fiery giant and then the gods Tyr, Thor and Heimdall all win battles of single combat, but die from their injuries – the latter in a fight to the death with Loki.

The entire earth submerges under water, and the nine worlds that the sons of Borr created are destroyed, before Midgard is repopulated by two mortals, Lif and Lifthrasir.

FINNISH MYTHOLOGY

One creation myth from Finland tells that the world was formed when the egg of a waterfowl exploded, with the top of the egg becoming the sky, supported by a pole which stretched from the North Star to the Earth. The Earth itself was believed to be flat, and at the edges of it was a land especially reserved for birds, called Lintukoto, which the birds travelled to along The Milky Way. Lintukoto was believed to be warm, and the birds visited it to escape the harsh northern European winters. Birds were also believed to bring the soul of a human being into his or her body at the moment of birth, and to take it away again at the moment of death.

RIVER TO THE UNDERWORLD

The underworld was called Tuonela, reached by crossing the river Tuoni, and all of the dead were believed to sleep there (the good were not taken to a 'heaven' as in so many other mythologies). A ferryman took the dead to their new home (there are clear parallels here to the figure of Charon, who ferried the dead across the river Acheron in Greek mythology). Shamans could reach Tuoni to seek the advice of the dead – but only if they could persuade the ferryman that they had a good reason.

The early pagan dwellers of Finland also believed bears were sacred animals, and it was forbidden to say the name of them for fear the bears would be offended and take revenge by scaring away the quarry of any hunter. Bears were seen by the Finns as the embodiment of their forefathers and were thus treated with the utmost respect.

THE KALEVALA

The central work of Finnish mythology is the Kalevala, an epic work of 50 interlinked poems compiled from traditional stories by Elias Lonnrot in the mid-19th century. Lonnrot spent 15 years collecting source material and also composed many lines of poetry himself in order to craft the disparate tales into a single, coherent story.

The central character of the Kalevala is Vainamoinen, god of songs and poetry, who spent so long in his mother's womb he was already an old man when he was born. He is a key figure in the Finnish creation myth. As he floats in a primordial ocean, an eagle's egg, laid on Vainamoinen's knee, falls and breaks open, the shell becoming the Earth and the sky, and the yoke the sun.

Much of the Kalevala deals with Vainamoinen's vain quest to find a wife. After he defeats the frost giant Joukahainen and buries him up to his neck in a bog, the giant offers his sister's hand in marriage to Vainamoinen in return for being released. However his sister Aino drowns herself rather than marry the old man.

LAND OF ICE GIANTS

Vainamoinen then journeys to Pohjola, the land of the ice giants, in order to try and find a wife. Louhi, the sorceress queen of Pohjola, offers him her daughter if he can create a magical device called a sampo, which brings good fortune to its owner and can produce endless quantities of gold and food. Vainamoinen persuades Ilmarinen, the blacksmith god, to produce the sampo, but Louhi's daughter sets him further impossible tasks, which Vainamoinen fails to achieve due to the intervention of malign spirits. Vainamoinen later steals the sampo back from Louhi, but she sends a storm that wrecks his ship and breaks the sampo into many pieces that are scattered across the world. Vainamoinen rescues some of the pieces and binds them together to ensure that spring will always defeat Louhi's attacks of cold weather.

Vainamoinen finally leaves the mortal realm in a boat he has fashioned from copper. In a passage of text with clear parallels with the Arthurian legend, he pledges to return should his homeland ever need him in the future.

SLAVIC MYTHOLOGY

Perhaps the most important god in Slavic mythology is Perun (or Peroon), the god of thunder and lightning, who features in more tales than any other deity. Perun comes down from the sky and does battle with Veles (or Volos), the god of the underworld, after Veles steals Perun's cattle. After a fierce battle, Perun drives Veles underground by firing lightning bolts (formed, in some accounts, from golden apples) at him. Having defeated Veles, Perun returns to the top of a world tree, the body of which represents the Earth, with the roots representing the underworld. Perun is sometimes symbolized as a bird (usually an eagle) perched at the top of the tree, with Veles a serpent coiled around the roots. The parallels with the Norse world tree, Yggdrasil, are striking.

In some accounts, both Perun and Veles are married to the sun, and share their wife's affections – Perun enjoying his wife's company during the day, and Veles at night. Storms were thought to be re-enactments of the battle between Perun and Veles, with the rain representing the restoration of order after Perun's victory.

Veles is also associated with trickery, and in a later Russian legend *The Tale of Igor's Campaign* (sometimes *The Song of Igor's Campaign*), a magician bard called Boyan

is referred to as the grandson of Veles. In the tale Prince Igor is drawn into a battle in which the odds are overwhelmingly against him, but after his inevitable defeat he manages to escape from his captors and returns to his homeland. The story remains one of the most popular legends in modern-day Russia.

According to the Christian missionaries who forcibly converted the pagan Slavs of Eastern Europe, one of their most sacred places was Radegast, a holy city where many gods were worshipped at a great temple. Some sources state that Radegast was in fact the name of a god (of hospitality and fertility) but the earliest source suggests that the main god worshipped at Radegast was Svarog, a Slavic sun god.

FIRE SNAKE

Svarog was often depicted as a fiery serpent, and the Slavs believed he was responsible for giving humankind the gift of fire, which was considered sacred within their culture. Fire was thus treated with great respect and it was taboo to shout at or curse a fire that refused to light. Earlier tales of Svarog describe him as a blacksmith, who caught the evil serpent (or multi-headed dragon), Zmey, with his tongs. Svarog uses the captured Zmey to pull a plough, and with this plough creates a divide between the world of the living and the world of the dead. Zmey is given the world of the dead to rule over, while Svarog reigns over the land of the living.

The Greek historian Herodotus recorded the strange tale of the Neuri tribe, who it is said lived around 500 BCE in what is now modern-day Belarus and Eastern Poland.

Herodotus mentions that according to legend, the Neuri turn into wolves once a year. Tales of werewolves are common in Slavic folklore, and this may be an early example of such a tale. The Neuri were all said to be wizards, and the legend may have grown from shamanistic rituals which often involve wearing animal skins.

TATAR MYTHOLOGY

The Tatars migrated west from the Gobi into Russia and Eastern Europe, bringing with them a unique culture and set of mythologies, some of which have survived to the present day. The Tatar writer, Gabdullah Tukai, wrote a story based upon the legend of Shurale which has since become famous amongst the Tatar.

THE FOREST DEMONS

Shurale is said to be a demon who lives in forests. He has a furry body, elongated fingers and a horn in the centre of his forehead. Shurale lures unwary travellers into undergrowth, where he uses his long fingers to tickle them to death. In Tukai's story, a woodcutter gets the better of Shurale by trapping his fingers in a log which he has been splitting. The woodcutter tells Shurale that his name is Last Year, and because Shurale shouts 'My fingers hurt! Last year!', none of his fellow forest dwellers come to help him. This has clear parallels with the story of Odysseus, who tells the Cyclops that his name is Nobody.

Other forest-dwelling spirits in Tatar myths include Seka, a dwarf who is often presented as a comic figure, and Abada, a benign spirit who resembles an old woman in appearance.

Siberian Tatars have their own forest-dwelling spirit, though he often prefers to inhabit derelict buildings. Pitsen is closely related to the figure of Shurale, but is believed to be able to turn himself into any shape he chooses, including the shape of a beautiful woman. He uses this form to seduce male travellers and copulate with them, or marry them.

ABOVE: An engraving of a Kazan Tatar couple in traditional dress, anon, Russia, 1889.

MYTHOLOGY OF THE LOWLANDS

Holland's most famous legendary export is the ghost ship *The Flying Dutchman*, which mariners have claimed to have seen at sea since at least the 18th century. The ship is said to be a Dutch man-of-war, doomed to sail the oceans for eternity. In some versions of the legend, the ship was cursed because the Captain made a deal with the devil (or played dice with the devil), though other versions suggest that the crew became infected with plague and no port would accept them. Most common is the notion that *The Flying Dutchman* was lost off the Cape of Good Hope in a storm which her sister ship survived. When her sister ship returned to the same spot after a refit, another storm raged and *The Flying Dutchman* reappeared, disappearing when the storm subsided.

SISTER BEATRIJS

The 14th century Dutch poem *Beatrijs* tells the legend of a nun who leaves her convent after falling in love with a man. She has two children with him before he abandons her after seven years. She turns to prostitution to support her children for another seven years. She then returns to the convent and enquires if they remember Sister Beatrijs. The nuns of the convent tells her that Sister Beatrijs has been in the convent for the entire 14 year period. It transpires that Mary, the mother of Jesus, has given Beatrijs a chance to return to the convent without anyone knowing she ever left – a chance Beatrijs takes.

ABOVE: Late 19th century wood engraving of the ghost ship *The Flying Dutchman*.

SAINT NICHOLAS

It is from the story of Saint Nicholas (via the Dutch *Sinterklass*) that the legend of Santa Claus or Father Christmas arose. As a famous bringer of gifts, he is celebrated on Saint Nicholas Day (usually December 6, his supposed birthday) in countries across the European mainland, where the festival is considered more important than Christmas day.

In Bari, Italy, where he is believed to be buried, the relics of the saint are taken out on a boat once a year in May. Elsewhere the celebration is usually marked by the giving of gifts, particularly to children.

BLACK PETES

In Holland, Belgium and parts of Germany, children leave their shoes out on Saint Nicholas's Eve (December 5), and in the morning find them magically filled with gifts – if they have been well behaved. If Sinterklass himself is seen, he is wearing a red bishop's robe and carrying a mitre, and often has companion Black Petes, or Zwarte Pieten, in tow. These are his mischievous helpers, in colourful Moorish dress dating back two centuries. If any of the children are found to have been naughty in the previous year, the legend states that the Black Petes will put them in a sack and take them to Spain. In many parts of Germany Saint Nicholas himself is believed to take badly behaved children away in a sack, while in Switzerland he beats them with a stick. In Croatia, Hungary and Romania he leaves a rod with the parents so that they can beat the children themselves.

ABOVE: 19th century illustration of St. Nicholas, the model for Santa Claus.

BASQUE MYTHOLOGY AND LEGENDS

Little of the ancient indigenous Basque mythology survived the arrival of Christianity, but records do exist of two of their major deities, the goddess Mari and her husband Sugaar (sometimes Maju). Mari was closely associated with the weather in Basque belief – it was said that when she travelled with Sugaar hail would fall, and that spells of wet or dry weather were as a result of her dwelling in different caves on a mountain. When she left one mountain cave for another there would be droughts or storms. She is often depicted as a woman of fire, or wearing red, with a full moon behind her head.

Mari's husband Sugaar is depicted as a dragon or serpent (Sugaar translates as male serpent). Very few myths surrounding him survive, and a legend indicating that he fathered the first Lord Of Biscay after seducing a Scottish princess is thought to be a much later story used to legitimize Biscay as a state in its own right.

OLENTZERO

The legend of Olentzero is one of the most popular in the modern day Basque region, with strong parallels to Santa Claus and Saint Nicholas (see page 63). Olentzero was said to be the last of a race of giants – jentilak – who once lived in the Pyrenees. Adopted by a family living in the woods, he grew up to be a fine carver of wood, and used his skills to make wooden toys that he would take to the children in the local village. When Olentzero died saving a child from a fire, a fairy granted him eternal life so that he could continue to bring his gifts to the children, which he is said to do in the middle of the night December 24 each year.

THE GREEN MAN

The mysterious figure of The Green Man occurs in cultures across the world, but is particularly common in Britain and Western European countries (Germany, France, Italy and Spain). Whilst none of the original legends of The Green Man have survived, the sheer volume of Green Man carvings that still exist attest to the fact that he was once an important figure in the ancient pagan belief system. From the 11th century onwards, many of the carvings are found in churches, abbeys and other places of religious observance, suggesting that the figure was subsumed within Christianity. In Britain, the figure became popular with the architects of the Gothic revival in the 19th century and the face of the Green Man adorns many buildings that date from this period.

WILD MAN OF THE WOODS

The Green Man is generally pictured as a wild man of the woods, with foliage sprouting from his mouth and nostrils. Often his entire face is covered with branches or vines, and in some representations these bear flowers or fruits.

Frequently his hair and beard are made of leaves. He would appear to be some form of nature spirit, and may have represented the rebirth of nature brought about by spring, and the concept of resurrection in general.

Similar images have been found in the Middle East and across much of Asia, though they are much less common than they are in Europe. Green Woman images are rare.

ABOVE: 'Green Man' stone carving, in the churchyard at St Mary de Crypt, Gloucester, UK.

PART 2
AFRICA & THE MIDDLE EAST

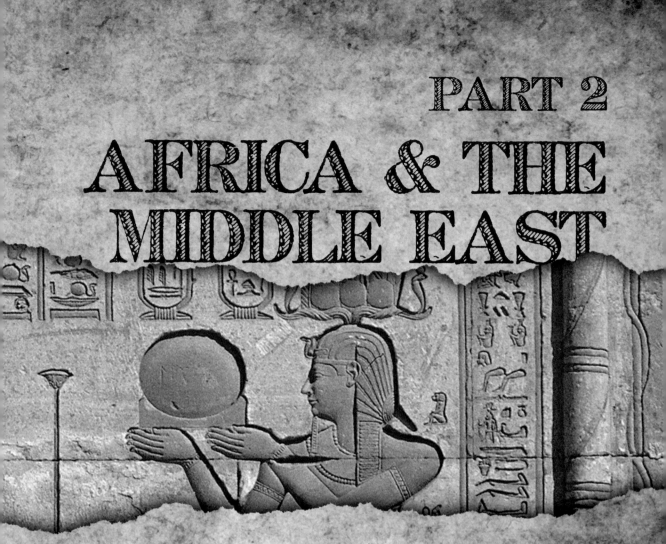

Grouped together in this section are myths and legends from the vast continent of Africa, and those from the birthplace of some of humanity's first great civilizations, The Middle East.

In ancient times, the mighty Sahara Desert served as a natural boundary that divided Africa into two distinct regions, with the northern region dominated by the ancient Egyptian Empire, and the southern region predominantly populated by a patchwork of smaller tribes and cultures. Contact between Egypt and the Middle Eastern kingdoms was regular, and many of the myths of the two regions share distinct similarities.

The same can not be said of the south, which remained a land largely unexplored until the 19th century. The sheer mystery of Africa for outsiders generated countless legends about the land – legends that were almost as fabulous as the gods and monsters of the indigenous people themselves.

ANCIENT EGYPT

The sophistication of the ancient Egyptian culture is truly astounding when we consider that many of the stories they set down were written some 5,000 years ago. Mysterious hieroglyphs that baffled experts for centuries were finally decoded in the 1820s and revealed a lost world of Pharaoh Kings and exotic deities. Many mysteries remain about ancient Egyptian culture, but the stories that have survived provide a unique insight into what was perhaps the most advanced ancient civilization on Earth.

EGYPTIAN CREATION MYTHS

The Egyptians actually had several different explanations for how the world came into being. In one version the world was woven by Neith, an ancient goddess of war and hunting, on her cosmic loom. Neith came into being spontaneously, and gave birth to the first god, Ra. She then strung the sky across her loom and wove the universe. Dipping her net into the primordial waters, she gathered up all the living creatures and placed them on the earth. Neith was said to be capable of unpicking the great tapestry of the universe if her offspring ever displeased her.

In another story the world was created by the sun god of Heliopolis, Atum. He later became associated with the great sun god Ra (or Re), as Atum-Ra. Creation was also associated with Khepri, the scarab or dung-beetle god, who was said to push the sun across the sky.

Most of the myths seem to agree that before the world there existed nothing but a vast primordial ocean called Nun

ABOVE: *Sacrifice by Priest for God Re-Horakhty*, painting on wood, Deir el Bahari, Luxor, Egypt, circa 900 BCE.

(sometimes Nu). Atum-Ra created himself out of this nothingness (as a shining egg in some versions), and then mated with himself to create a son (Shu) and daughter (Tefnut). In some versions of the myth Atum-Ra spits out his son and vomits his daughter. In others the offspring are produced by Atum-Ra masturbating into the void. The newly created god and goddess were associated with air (Shu) and moisture (Tefnut).

GEB AND NUT

Shu and Tefnut brought forth Geb and Nut. Geb and Nut were born entwined together in a tight sexual embrace, but they were then separated, with Nut being pushed upwards to form the sky and Geb downwards to form the earth. They gave birth to the gods Osiris, Isis, Set and Nephthys.

In some versions of the myths, mankind was created from the tears of joy that Atum-Ra wept when he found Shu and Tefnut, who had become lost. Ra is said to have become the first Pharaoh, ruling over Egypt for thousands of years, having taken human form so that mankind could worship him.

THE MYTH OF RA

Ra becomes angry with mankind because, in time, it had ceased to worship him, viewing him as an old man. He orders his daughter Sekhmet, a ferocious goddess who delights in blood and slaughter, to destroy all living humans. Seeing the river Nile turn red with blood, however, Ra takes pity on humanity and decides to save it. Powerless to stop the insatiable bloodlust of Sekhmet, he resorts to trickery, pouring ochre and beer into the

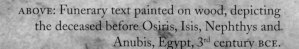

ABOVE: Funerary text painted on wood, depicting the deceased before Osiris, Isis, Nephthys and Anubis, Egypt, 3rd century BCE.

fields Sekhmet plans to visit next, so that the fields appear to be deep in blood. Sekhmet, seeing the red beer and believing it to be human blood, drinks deeply and becomes drunk. In her stupor she can no longer kill, and thus the rest of humankind is saved from destruction.

OSIRIS AND ISIS

Two of the children of Geb and Nut, Osiris and Isis were married to each other (a common practice amongst Pharaohs). Osiris ruled over the land as king after his father Ra had departed back to the heavens. He introduced farming to Egypt, and the people became prosperous and happy. One Egyptian myth tells of how his brother Set became jealous of Osiris's position, and plotted to dethrone him.

Whilst Osiris is away and Isis is ruling in his place, Set builds a chest from rare and valuable materials, made to exactly fit Osiris's body. On Osiris's return, Set and his 72 co-conspirators organize a huge feast, with Osiris as guest of honour. The wondrous chest is brought into the room and Set offers to give it to whomever it best fits. After the co-conspirators all lie in the chest and find it does not fit them, Osiris tries lying in it, and Set slams the lid shut before sealing the whole chest with molten lead. The chest is then thrown into the river Nile, and Osiris is drowned.

THE SEARCH FOR OSIRIS

Isis goes in search of her husband's body, and finds that the chest has been washed down to Byblos (in modern day Lebanon), where it has become embedded in the trunk of a cedar tree. She is told that the tree has since been used to construct a pillar in a palace for the King and Queen of Byblos.

Isis manages to break open the pillar without damaging the palace, and returns to Egypt with Osiris's body, where she buries him in secret – either in marshes or in the desert, depending on the story.

Set discovers the whereabouts of Osiris's grave and exhumes his body before dismembering it into 14 parts. He scatters the parts across the lands of Egypt. Nephthys, the wife and sister of Set, leaves Set to help Isis track down the 14 parts of Osiris's body to resurrect him. They manage to find all of the pieces except for Osiris's penis, which has been eaten by a crocodile (or, in some versions of the story, a carp). Isis makes a likeness of the penis using magic (the words required being supplied by the god Thoth, discussed later), and uses it to impregnate herself and give birth to a son, Horus.

JOURNEY TO THE UNDERWORLD

Osiris, now whole again, travels to the underworld (Amenti) where he becomes the god who sits in judgement on the dead. From this point on, Osiris becomes associated with death and rebirth, including the flooding and retreating of the river Nile. In time he would grow to be perhaps the most important of all Egyptian deities.

Horus battles Set and manages to defeat him, and later becomes known as the god of the sky. The battle between Horus and Set may be an echo of the period when Egypt was divided into two separate kingdoms in the north and south. Many deities which were worshipped separately in the north and south may well have been given new relationships to one another when Egypt was unified. The creation of these new relationships is what appears to have spurred the Egyptians to generate myths.

THOTH

Usually regarded as the son of Ra – though some claim he was the son of Set, and born from his father's forehead – Thoth was the ancient Egyptian god of writing, and also of magic. He acted as the scribe and record keeper to the gods and was responsible for the invention of hieroglyphs. It was through Thoth that the gods made themselves known to mankind, so he was one of the most respected gods in the Egyptian pantheon.

In many stories Thoth plays the role of mediator, ensuring that good and evil are in balance and that no single god can ever take full control of the world. He watches over three great battles between good and evil, healing any god who appears mortally wounded. He plays a crucial role in the story of Isis and Osiris, providing the incantations that resurrect Osiris and allow him to impregnate Isis.

360 DAYS A YEAR

Thoth also plays a prominent role in one of the more memorable ancient Egyptian myths, concerning the creation of the 365-day calendar. The story begins in a time when there were only 360 days in a year. Nut, the goddess of the sky, is made pregnant by Geb, the earth, which angers Ra. He pushes the two of them apart and curses Nut so that she will be unable to give birth to her children on any day of any month.

Thoth consoles Nut but also knows, in his role as god of magic, that Ra's curse cannot be undone. However he manages to find an ingenious solution to her problem. He invents the game of draughts, and gambles with the moon at the game for a stake of one seventieth of her 360 days of light. Thoth wins, and weaves the portions of moonlight into five new days (360 days divided by 70 = 5). The extra five days in the year allow Nut to give birth to five children (Osiris, Horus, Set, Isis and Nepthys). The moon's light dwindles at certain times because of it losing five days worth of light to Thoth.

Thoth is generally depicted with the head of a baboon or ibis. His name translates as 'He who is like an ibis', and in the form of a baboon he was said to sit in judgement on the dead, recording the weight of their souls. He is also often shown holding up a crescent moon. Vast numbers of dead ibis were killed and mummified in Thoth's honour in the later ancient Egyptian period.

The ancient Greeks equated Thoth with their own god Hermes, and credited him with the authorship of every work of ancient wisdom. One cult of Greek worshippers believed that the books of Thoth were guarded by his priests, and that within the pages of these books lay all the knowledge in the world. They renamed the Egyptian town of Khmun, the centre of Thoth's cult, as Hermopolis, meaning 'city of Hermes'.

ABOVE: Ptolemaic temple of Horus, Edfu, Egypt.

THE EYE OF HORUS

One of the most prevalent symbols in ancient Egyptian tombs and temples and on ancient Egyptian amulets, is the Eye of Horus (or Udjat, sometimes called the Eye of Ra). It symbolizes protection and power, and was used to ward off evil spirits. Ancient Egyptian sailors would often paint the Eye of Horus on the bow of their ships to try and ensure safe passage across the seas.

Horus was often depicted as a falcon or hawk, and thus the Eye of Horus usually has hawk-like markings, sometimes with a teardrop beneath the eye. In his battle with the evil Set, Horus lost his left eye which Set then tore apart. The eye was healed by Thoth (god of wisdom and learning), or, in some versions, by Hathor (goddess of love and wife of Horus), and returned to Horus. The left eye symbolized the moon to ancient Egyptians, with the right eye symbolizing the sun. Amulets depicting the Eye of Horus have been found wrapped in the bandages of Egyptian mummies, particularly near to the incisions made by the embalmers.

Representations of eyes are common in many belief systems, though their meaning varies from culture to culture. The concept of an 'all-seeing eye' appears in Buddhism and is a symbol on modern American one dollar banknotes. The image of an 'evil eye' has been found on Greco-Roman drinking vessels and upon artefacts from countless other cultures across the world. Often the power of the 'evil eye' could be warded off with amulets or talismans.

ABOVE: Pectoral of the sacred eye flanked by the serpent goddess of the North and the vulture goddess of the South, made from gold cloisonne with glass-paste, from the tomb of the pharaoh Tutankhamun.

ANCIENT EGYPTIAN UNDERWORLD AND AFTERLIFE

Maps have been found painted on the floors of coffins that give a detailed guide to the journey that ancient Egyptian rulers expected to make after death. Known as *The Book of Two Ways* these maps suggest two alternative routes for the dead to take (one via water, and one via land) in order to reach paradise. They also include spells and incantations that the dead will need to get past various obstacles along the way.

FIELD OF OFFERINGS

The Egyptians imagined the underworld as divided into numerous caverns, each with a gate and a guardian. The dead had to find their way through this underworld, which was equated with the night sky, in order to reach paradise, where they would sit amongst the stars. In one part of the underworld (Rosetau), Osiris waits in a room with walls of fire. If the deceased prove themselves worthy of eternal life, they will be granted entry to the Field of Offerings, a heavenly paradise. The heart of the deceased is weighed against a feather, that represents the goddess of truth, Maat. If the heart is heavy with sin then it is devoured by a monster.

The famous Egyptian *Book of the Dead* was just one of a whole series of manuals designed to assist the dead in their journey through the underworld. Copies of it have been found in tombs all across ancient Egypt, usually written on papyrus. It contains some 200 spells which the dead may need to help them find their way into paradise.

ABOVE: Fragment of the Egyptian *Book of the Dead*.

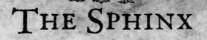

THE SPHINX

The most famous Sphinx is the one that lies facing due East in front of the Great Pyramid at Giza, but sphinxes were actually relatively common in ancient Egypt, appearing to have been used as guardian figures for tombs and temples. They consist of the body of a lion with the head or face of a human being. In the case of the Great Sphinx at Giza, the face is believed to be that of the Pharaoh Khafra, who ruled some time around 2500 BCE. Exactly what the lion-man represented, or how it protected the Pharaohs, remains unknown.

MYSTERIOUS CONSTRUCTION

The name 'Sphinx' was first ascribed to the monuments by the ancient Greeks, who had close contact with the Egyptians and included a Sphinx in one of their myths. This Sphinx is the one that famously asks the riddle 'Which creature has four legs in the morning, two in the day time and three in the evening?' – the answer to which (man) was provided by Oedipus. This should not be confused with the other 'riddle of the Sphinx' which relates to the origin and purpose of the Great Sphinx of Giza monument itself. Remarkably few inscriptions relating to the construction of the monument have been found, and those that have survived appear to have been inscribed long after the Great Sphinx was erected. The fact that the Egyptians had so little to say about such a staggering monument has given rise to numerous legends and wild theories about the Sphinx.

THE INVENTORY STELA

One artefact, the Inventory Stela, found at a nearby temple, appears to suggest that the Pharaoh Khufu discovered the Great Sphinx buried in the sand, and organized its restoration. This would make the monument considerably older than previously thought. It has also been suggested that erosion patterns on the body of the Great Sphinx are consistent with water damage, rather than wind damage, and that this is proof that it was built by an unknown ancient civilization before a catastrophic flood obliterated their culture. There have been no significant rainfalls in the area since around 4000 BCE. However most scientific experts reject these and the numerous other theories that point away from the widely agreed upon date for the construction of the Great Sphinx of around 2500 BCE.

The oldest human-animal sculpture found to date also blends the features of a man and a lion. It is the so-called 'lion man' figurine found in the German cave of Hohlenstein Stadel, and is thought to be around 32,000 years old. Similar half-human and half-lion figures exist in the mythologies of many Asian cultures. In India, images of man-beasts are said to take away the sins of those entering temples and are thus often found beside gateways and entrances. The image of the sphinx has also been adopted widely in Masonic architecture, representing secret ancient wisdom.

ABOVE: The Great Sphinx of Giza, nr. Cairo, Egypt.

THE CURSE OF TUTANKHAMUN

Legends of cursed Egyptian tombs have circulated for many years, and perhaps the most famous of them all is the Curse Of Tutankhamun, which evolved after Howard Carter's discovery of Tutankhamun's tomb in 1922. In truth, much of the story was invented or exaggerated by the press in order to sell newspapers (Carter signed an exclusive deal with *The Times*, and so other papers had to find their own angle). The rumours of a curse began after the death of Lord Carnarvon, who had financed Carter's expedition to Egypt. Carnarvon slashed open an old mosquito bite whilst shaving, and died of blood poisoning in 1923. There had earlier been reports of Carter's pet canary being eaten by a cobra, which was taken to be a bad omen and proof of a supernatural force at work. The Uraeus, a spitting cobra in an upright position, was a symbol commonly found in ancient Egypt, including upon Tutankhamun's famous death mask. It represented divine authority.

Additional details to the story of Carnarvon's death were soon added: it was reported that his dog had let out a long howl and fallen over dead at the same time as her master died. The lights of Cairo were also have said to have gone out shortly after Carnarvon's death.

SPOOKY INSCRIPTION

Press reports suggested that the words 'Death shall come on swift wings to he who disturbs the peace of the king' were inscribed in Tutankhamun's tomb, but in fact there was no such curse, and inscribed curses are relatively rare in Egyptian tombs. Some curses do appear in Old Kingdom tombs (dating to around 2500 BCE) but for the most part Egyptians did not appear to even consider the possibility that a grave would be disturbed. Such curses seem to have been aimed at the priests tending the tombs, reminding them to do their work well, rather than being aimed at grave robbers. Many inscriptions do claim to offer protection for the deceased, and such an inscription was found in Tutankhamun's tomb, but the protection is from the forces of nature and the forces of the supernatural, and no threat was made to take revenge on a person disturbing the remains.

The deaths of anyone who had any sort of association with the tomb were blamed on the ongoing curse, but the statistics suggest there was no malign force at work. Carter himself lived until 1939, dying at the age of 64, having spent some 10 years working in the tomb. Dr D.E. Derry, who carried out the autopsy on Tutankhamun and might have been considered a prime target of any curse, lived to the age of 86.

In theory it is possible that bacteria, moulds and toxic gases could accumulate in old tombs and cause those entering physical harm. However in most cases a strong odour would alert a person to the presence of poisonous fumes.

ABOVE: Canopic coffin from Tutankhamun's
tomb.

THE
MIDDLE EAST

In ancient times, Egypt and the cultures of North Africa had closer ties to the Middle Eastern region than they did to the rest of Africa, so it is perhaps not surprising that we find many parallels between the myths of these two regions. However, whilst the myths of ancient Egypt remained relatively insular, ancient Sumerian, Babylonian, and Assyrian myths became gradually assimilated into the monotheistic religions which in time came to dominate the region – Christianity, Judaism and Islam.

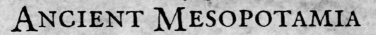

ANCIENT MESOPOTAMIA

The ancient kingdom of Mesopotamia, which occupied the region between the Tigris and Euphrates Rivers (now modern day Iraq), saw the rise of the world's first true cities and farming cultures, some of which date back 5,000 years. As a great trading nation, the peoples of Mesopotamia had contacts with numerous other cultures, and the stories that they told eventually spread throughout Persia, Egypt and into mainland Europe.

The myths from Mesopotamia are an amalgamation of tales from the Sumerian, Babylonian, Akkadian and Assyrian cultures. Throughout the long history of Mesopotamia the myths evolved, and the worshipped deities shifted from abstract spirits to gods that took a more human form. Local cities or cults developed their own versions of the core myths, and often the names and representations of gods varied from region to region. In time, the kings of Mesopotamia described themselves as gods, becoming deified when they ascended to the throne.

ABOVE: Relief representing men paying tributes, from the Palace of Sargon II, Khorsabad, Iraq, circa 722-705 BCE.

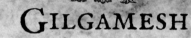

GILGAMESH

It appears that Gilgamesh himself was a real historical figure, a king of Uruk who is thought to have ruled around 2700 BCE. Some of the earliest Sumerian texts give his name as Bilgames. His father was said to be a demon who took the form of the King of Uruk, and his mother was the goddess Ninsun or Ninsuna (lady wild cow). Gilgamesh is portrayed as a figure of superhuman strength, two-thirds god and one-third man.

EPIC BATTLE

Exhausted after building the great walls of the city of Uruk on Gilgamesh's command, the citizens of the city cry out to the father of the gods (Anu) for help. He sends Enkidu, a wild man who lives in the forest with the animals, to Uruk. Gilgamesh and Enkidu fight an epic battle, in the course of which each comes to respect the other's power. Enkidu teaches the tyrannical Gilgamesh the nature of kindness, mercy and compassion, and the two become as close as brothers.

Inspired by a dream, Gilgamesh decides to journey to the sacred realm of the Cedar Forest to kill the guardian of the forest, the demon Humbaba. Enkidu fails to dissuade Gilgamesh from this venture, and eventually pledges to join him. The citizens of Uruk secretly hope that the demon will kill them both, but Gilgamesh and Enkidu slay Humbaba and return to Uruk triumphant.

PREMONITION OF MURDER

Gilgamesh then rejects the sexual advances of the goddess of love and war, Ishtar. Enraged, she asks her father Anu to send the bull of heaven down to Uruk to kill Gilgamesh. The bull kills many innocent people before Gilgamesh and Enkidu manage to capture it and tear out its heart. The people of Uruk celebrate, but Enkidu has a dream in which he foresees the gods murdering him as revenge for the deaths of Humbaba and the bull. He is then stricken with an illness sent by the gods, and after his death a grief-stricken Gilgamesh resolves to set out to discover the secrets of immortality from Utnapishtum. His wife and the mortals chosen by the gods to survive the great flood then enjoy everlasting life.

Gilgamesh's journey to the distant realm of Dilmun, where Utnapishtum now lives, is an epic adventure story which sees him overcome numerous obstacles and defeat all manner of monsters before arriving at his destination. There, Utnapishtum reprimands him for seeking to overcome death, and explains that death is integral to life for human beings and attempting to defy the gods is futile. Utnapishtum tests Gilgamesh's conviction by challenging him to stay awake for seven nights – a test which Gilgamesh promptly fails. When he awakes, Utnapishtum banishes him back to Uruk, but tells him of a flower which grows at the bottom of the ocean and which has the power to restore his youth.

RETURN TO URUK

Gilgamesh manages to find and retrieve the flower, but it is eaten by a serpent, who thus obtains the ability to shed his skin. A despondent Gilgamesh returns to Uruk, where the sight of the mighty walls he constructed remind him that this will be the way he achieves immortality, as no one will ever forget who was responsible for such a mighty construction.

One version of the story ends with Enkidu returning from the dead, but this is believed to be a much later addition to the main tale. Some stories tell of Gilgamesh being buried beneath the river Euphrates, which was diverted by the people of Uruk for this purpose.

FLOODS IN GILGAMESH AND OTHER ANCIENT TALES

At 5,000 years old, the epic tale of Gilgamesh is one of the very oldest stories to survive to modern times. The cuneiform tablets which relate the tale tell of a cataclysmic flood sent by god to destroy mankind – and there is a clear parallel here with the biblical flood of Genesis. Indeed stories of great floods appear in countless mythologies, and it remains unclear whether they all stem from Gilgamesh, have appeared separately, or have an alternative common source which has since been lost to us. Experts believe that the prevalence of flood stories points to a real disaster that occurred in ancient times, and that the diverse stories may be the result of different cultures recording a single worldwide event. In most versions of the story one chosen human being is warned by god of the coming disaster, and survives the devastation to repopulate the world.

ABOVE: Babylonian bas-relief showing Gilgamesh pursuing demon.

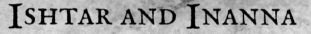

ISHTAR AND INANNA

Ishtar was the ancient Babylonian goddess of sex, and Inanna was her ancient Sumerian counterpart. Each culture had a very similar myth of the goddess journeying to the underworld – a common theme in mythology, as we have already seen.

Both Ishtar and Inanna were said to be highly fertile, but each had a single main love – Tammuz in the case of Ishtar, and Dumuzi in the case of Inanna. Ishtar's reason for visiting the underworld is to restore her dead lover back to life, whereas Inanna goes there to visit her sister, Erishkigal (it is not clear what prompts her to want to visit Erishkigal). Both Ishtar and Inanna set off wearing their finest robes and regalia. As they travel through seven gates to reach the underworld, they are each forced to remove an item of clothing if they wish to pass. The result is that in both versions of the myth the goddess arrives at her destination naked. In the case of the Babylonian Ishtar, her sister Erishkigal is furious that Ishtar wishes to free her lover from the underworld, and so she imprisons Ishtar and tortures her mercilessly. In the Sumerian version Inanna is assumed by the judges of the underworld to have come to take her sister's place, and she is dragged off and hung upon a butcher's hook until she rots.

TRICKSTER GOD

In both versions of the myth, the fact that the goddess of fertility and sex is trapped in the underworld has terrible consequences on earth. There is no light, sex or fertility, so the gods decide that Ishtar/Inanna must be released. A trickster god is asked to create a mortal (or three zombie-like beings in the Sumerian version) who is sent down to the underworld to rescue the goddess. The exact details of the rescue differ from version to version,

ABOVE: Statue of Ishtar wearing a headdress, from the Temple of Ushtar, Mari (Tell Hariri), Syria, 2800–2300 BCE.

but in both stories the rescue is ultimately successful and fertility is restored to the earth.

There is a sting in the tale for the goddesses's lovers, however. In the case of Ishtar, her beloved Tammuz remains in the underworld and is only allowed to escape once a year to see her – which is the cause of Spring. Whenever they meet, Ishtar's passion is so great that it destroys Tammuz after six months, and so he must return to the underworld – which is the cause of Winter.

Inanna, in contrast, discovers that her lover Dumuzi did not mourn for her when she was away, and so she orders him to take her place in the underworld. He too is allowed to return to earth to meet with his lover once a year for six months to ensure that fertility remains on the earth. Dumuzi thus came to be considered a god of vegetation in Sumerian mythology.

PERSIAN MYTHOLOGY

The central text of Persian mythology is the *Shahnameh*, or *Book of Kings*, written in the 10th century by the Persian poet Ferdowsi. It recounts the history of Persia (broadly the land now known to us as Iran) from the beginning of time to the Islamic conquest in the 7th century. It reflects the religion of ancient Persia, Zoroastrianism, in that all of the deities described are either good or evil, as in Zoroastrianism the two have very distinct and separate sources. The book is divided into three main parts – the Mythical Age, the Heroic Age and the Historical Age.

Within the section that deals with the Mythical Age lies a Persian version of the creation myth seen in so many other cultures. Ahura Mazda, the supreme god, creates 16 lands on the earth. As he finishes each land, the devil Angra Mainyu (or Ahriman) introduces an evil trait to each one. Subsequently human beings live on the earth. These humans at first live in caves and wear leopard skins, until one of them, Keyumars, rises to the status of king, or shah. His son Siyamak is challenged in battle by the son of Angra Mainyu, and killed. However Siyamak's son Hushang (or Hoshang) kills the demon's son in a later battle and claims the throne, ruling as the second shah. Hushang is said to have introduced many technologies to the world, including fire, which he discovered after hurling a flint rock at a serpent. The flint missed the serpent and struck another rock, producing a spark, which in turn created fire. One of modern Iran's most important mid-winter festivals, the Sadeh (sometimes Sade or Sada), celebrates this event.

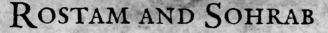

ROSTAM AND SOHRAB

Rostam is a legendary warrior in Persian mythology, immortalized in the *Shahnameh* and described there as the son of Zal and Rudabeh. Zal was abandoned as a child and reared by a magical bird (the Simorgh), and Rudabeh was descended from a serpent (Zohak, who had to be fed on human brains). Their unlikely romance includes a moment when Rudabeh offers to let down her hair so that Zal can use it as a rope to climb into her tower. Rostam is born by caesarean after Zal summons the Simorgh to assist with the difficult birth. He is said to have been born the size of a lion cub, and grew to the size of a man within a few weeks.

As a man-sized child, Rostam displays prodigious strength, killing a rampaging white elephant with a single blow and taming the wild stallion Rakhsh, the horse he would later ride on his epic adventures. Rakhsh is the only horse strong enough to carry Rostam's powerful frame, and his loyalty to his master was famed across Persia.

SEVEN TRIALS

Once grown, Rostam, riding upon Rakhsh, embarks on seven heroic trials to free the king Kavus from demons. The warrior and his horse act as a team, with Rakhsh saving the sleeping Rostam from a lion in their first adventure. They then survive a daunting trip through a vast desert, slay a dragon and a witch before facing the mighty hero Ulad and his army. Rostam kills Ulad's entire army single-handedly, and Ulad recognizes his greatness and offers to guide him on his travels. Rostam and Rakhsh then defeat the demon king before rescuing King Kavus from his castle, which is besieged by demons.

When Rakhsh is stolen from Rostam, he journeys to the King of Samangan to ask for his help. The king offers him shelter, and in the night the king's daughter Tahmina comes to his chamber and pledges her love for him. They make love, and Rostam gives Tahmina a bracelet, telling her to give it to their child if she falls pregnant. She does indeed become pregnant, and gives birth to a son, Sohrab.

SOHRAB'S SECRET

When Sohrab grows up, he demands to know who his father is and Tahmina tells him, begging him to keep it a secret. Sohrab is sent to war, not knowing that the man he will face in battle is his father Rostam. The two fight and Sohrab has the opportunity to kill his father but allows him to live when Rostam tells him the laws of battle dictate that he must be felled three times before being killed.

In due course Rostam kills Sohrab, who reveals his identity as he lies dying, and tells of his love for his father. Rostam, heartbroken, burns his armour and builds his son a golden tomb. Tahmina, when learning of her son's death, dies of grief.

RIGHT: Sohrab looking at Rostam's green tent, from a 16th century manuscript of *Shah-nameh*, by Firdausi (934-1020).

رسیدکان بیروبردہ سرا
چهارم ازسراپردہ سنبازسرایردہ رستم سبامہ دیگرکش
یکی لشکری کس بردہ بیای

زدہ بیش او اختر
یکی تخت برمایہ بہ اندر میان
ابا فرو باسفت وبال کوان
ازان کس کبریابیششتست

درشسته تکی پهلوان
نشسته بسان پیش رش برست
یکی سہ کبری پیش برست
یزدہ نیمہ ہی کس بہتای

SUB-SAHARAN AFRICA

Separated from the rest of Africa by the mighty Sahara desert, the civilizations of the south developed mythologies that are quite separate from those of Egypt and the Middle East. Christianity came relatively late to the south, and even after the first missionaries arrived, belief in more ancient spirits persisted. No one set of myths unites this vast continent, home to countless cultures and thousands of languages, though some common themes do emerge. A belief in an afterlife is more or less universal, as is the belief in a single supreme god (though the name and shape of that god differs greatly). In most African cultures the worship of ancestors forms a key part of the religious belief system, and rituals are performed to ensure that the ancestors are kept placated. The retelling of stories may have formed part of the early rituals.

AFRICAN CREATION MYTHS

The majority of the myths were not written down until modern times, as the tradition of most African cultures was predominantly oral, with tales being told or sung by specialized storytellers. For this reason it is difficult to determine how old most African myths really are, but the likelihood is that their roots stretch back to the very distant past. The core myths of many African tribes relate to who created the world, and why. Many of the myths tell of humans being originally destined for immortality, but later being reduced to the status of mortals. The creation myths often describe how one god came to rule over all of the others, though it often seems that lesser gods were more important to the day-to-day lives of humans than the supreme god. Sometimes the same god features in quite contradictory stories in different cultures, with gods becoming goddesses on more than one occasion, and many gods being portrayed as tricksters or usurpers. It is thus difficult to summarize the key attributes of African deities, but what follows are the most widely held beliefs relating to the more popular mythical figures.

BAKUBA PEOPLE

For the Bakuba people, the earth began as an endless expanse of water and darkness, ruled by Mbombo, a great white giant. Mbombo feels a terrible pain in his stomach, and vomits twice to create all that is known in the world. The first time he vomits, the sun, moon and stars emerge. The heat of the sun causes the water on earth to evaporate and form the clouds. The second time he vomits, humans, animals and everything else in the world emerges.

THE MASSAI

The creator made three sons from a tree that had split into three pieces, is a belief held by the Massai of Kenya. He sends his three sons out to live in the wild, where they become the first fathers of their people. To the Massai father he gives a stick, to the Kikuyu father he gives a hoe and to the Kamba father he gives a bow and arrow. The Massai father uses the stick to tend cattle, the Kikuyu father uses the hoe to tend land, and the Kamba father uses the bow and arrow to hunt.

ZULU MYTHOLOGY

The creator god is called Unkulunkulu, in Zulu mythology, and he is said to have grown on a reed in the swamp that preceded the earth. The myth states that at first human beings had no words, and they only had to think of a desire in order to have it fulfilled. Later another set of gods creates language, and as soon as human beings can talk they begin to fall out with one another, and the myth informs us that they have been in conflict ever since.

AFRICAN VOODOO

The sky serpent Damballa makes all of the waters of the planet, and the movement of his coils creates mountains and valleys, according to African Voodoo beliefs. After shedding his skin in the heat of the sun, the waters of the world are released and they combine with the sun to form a rainbow. Damballa falls in love with the rainbow and makes her his wife.

THE ELEPHANT

s the largest animal in Africa, it is hardly surprising that the elephant makes appearances in numerous African myths and legends. It is usually portrayed as an intelligent, kindly, and trusting animal, who is often the victim of deceit or violence – frequently at the hands of man. One legend tells that the first elephant was the wife of a man who, seeking wealth, rubs a magic ointment on her teeth. Her teeth grow and grow and the man pulls them out and makes a great deal of money by selling the ivory. When his wife's teeth grow back even larger, however, she refuses to let him pull them out, and the rest of her body grows until she turns into an elephant and leaves him to live in the wild.

POISON ARROWS

Another myth tells that at first there was only one man, one elephant, and thunder on the earth. Thunder becomes afraid of man, because he can turn over in his sleep, which neither thunder nor the elephant can do. Fleeing to the sky, thunder warns the elephant to beware of mankind, but the elephant laughs because humans are so small in size compared to elephants. However the human makes a bow and shoots the elephant with poison arrows. As it lies dying the elephant calls out to the thunder to take it up into the sky, but the thunder refuses, reminding the elephant of its earlier warning about man. Man goes on to conquer all of the animals in the world.

THE CHAMELEON

One popular Zulu myth concerns how human beings became mortal – another common theme in mythologies from around the world. The story begins with a chameleon (sometimes called Unwaba) catching two human beings (a man and a woman) in its fishing net. As it has never seen a human being before, it takes the two humans to the god Mukungu and shows him what it has found.

Mukungu decides that humans should be allowed to live on earth in peace, and in time there are so many humans that the gods move from earth into the heavens to give themselves more space. The gods give a message to the chameleon to tell to the humans: that humans will rise from the dead whenever they die. However the chameleon is slow in delivering the message, and he is overtaken by a lizard who brings the message that human beings will not return when they die. This incorrect message is the reason human beings became mortal, and it is said that chameleons change colour because they are blushing at the chameleon's sloth.

In some versions of the story the lizard had been eavesdropping on the conversation that the gods had with the chameleon, and in his haste to be the first with the message he misunderstood the meaning. In many areas of Africa chameleons (and lizards in general) are feared and associated with bad luck even today, perhaps because of this story.

OLORUN AND OLOKUN

The gods have a competition to determine who is the most beautiful, and the main two contenders are the sky (Olorun, sometimes Olodumare) and the water (Olokun). In some versions of the story Olorun and Olokun are married, with the sky represented as male and the oceans and rivers as female, but in most versions both are male.

Olorun wins the contest because he demonstrates that Olokun's beauty is just a reflection of his own beauty. In some versions of the story the two gods have a weaving contest, which Olorun wins when Olokun realizes that even Olorun's humble messenger, the chameleon, can change his skin to match the most beautiful cloths she can conjure up.

Olorun then creates the land, trees and plants. Exactly how he achieves this again varies from culture to culture, but in at least one version he sends his son, the lesser god Oduduwa, down to earth with a cockerel, a pigeon and a container full of soil. Oduduwa scatters the soil across the waters, and the cockerel and pigeon scratch and scatter the soil to create all of the lands of the world. Plants and trees are then grown from seeds, and animals and human beings are moulded from clay.

IMMORTAL GIANTS

It is said that initially humans were immortal giants like the gods themselves, but Olokun realized that this meant they would one day challenge the gods and so he shrank humans to their present size, and made them mortal.

Whilst not considered a creator god like Olorun, Olokun nonetheless remained an important deity in the Yoruba belief system, particularly in Benin. Sometimes described as female, and the wife of Olorun, she is associated with wisdom as deep as the ocean and later became the patron deity of many Africans uprooted by the slave trade. Olokun translates as 'owner of oceans'.

One ritual that survives to the present day in Benin is a dance that celebrates the myth of Olokun and the hunter. In this story, a hunter chases a wild pig into the woods, and from there is taken down under the river Ethiope where he meets Olokun. He stays underwater for three years and learns a great deal of wisdom and magic from Olokun. When he returns to his village, carrying a pot of water upon his head, he has temporarily lost the power of speech and so begins to dance. His fellow villagers join in with his dance which lasts for 14 days. Finally the hunter begins to relate the story of what has happened to him, and to demonstrate the magic and healing powers that he has learnt. He is named as the chief priest of Olokun.

ABOVE: Statue of Shango, god of thunder.

MAWU AND LISA

The Fon people of Benin attach great importance to the female deity Mawu and the male deity Lisa, who are often referred to jointly as the androgynous deity 'Mawu-Lisa'. They are the offspring of the supreme deity Nana Buluku, with Mawu representing the moon and Lisa representing the sun. Mawu is also associated with the West (where he is said to dwell), with Lisa being associated with the East. Together they are believed to have created the world and all that it contains, in a period of four days.

In the myth, the universe and humanity are created on day one. On day two, Mawu-Lisa make the earth habitable for human beings. Mawu-Lisa then gave human beings their senses, and language, before finally giving them the gift of technology on the last day of creation.

IMPORTANT ROLES

The act of union between Mawu and Lisa is said to have occurred at the first solar eclipse, and in time the deity (or deities) produced offspring. Mawu-Lisa gathers their offspring together and gives them all roles in the world. To their first born twins they give the world and all its riches. Their next child remains in the sky, as it has both male and female forms, like Mawu-Lisa. To their next set of twins they give the oceans, and to their next child they give command of all the animals. Their next son is given the task of teaching humans how to live happily, and their next becomes the air, which men need to live.

Each of the offspring is given a language to speak, but the language of the gods is taken away from them. The very youngest, Legba, stays with Mawu-Lisa and is the only one who can speak all of the languages, plus the language of the gods. For this reason, the Fon people often ask Legba to provide for them and protect them, as he is the one who reports on the work of all of the others to Mawu-Lisa. Legba acts as a divine messenger relaying messages between the worlds of the humans and the spirits. In many African cultures this messenger spirit is known as Eshu. Capable of circling the entire world in an instant, Legba/Eshu is often portrayed as a trickster spirit who is not beyond using mischievous means to teach human beings a lesson or two. In some areas he is known by the nickname 'Aflakete' which translates roughly as 'I have tricked you'.

LEGBA'S TRICKERY

The most famous tale of Legba's trickery concerns two inseparable friends who had forgotten to pay respect to him. Legba walks along the dividing line of two adjacent fields that are owned and farmed by two friends, wearing a hat that is black on one side and white on the other. He makes small talk with both of the friends and then leaves. The friends discuss the stranger in the hat and begin to argue violently over whether he was wearing a black hat or a white hat. Legba returns to break up the ensuing fight between the friends, shows them the hat that is black on one side and white on the other, and reminds them to pay him due respect in future.

THE TOKOLOSHE

eared throughout southern Africa is the mythical Tokoloshe (or Tikoloshe or Teikolosha). In most cultures it is portrayed as a zombie-like dwarf, though in some cultures it is a worm-like creature with the head of a dog. Often it is stated that the Tokoloshe has a hole in its head. Some legends state that the Tokoloshe's penis is so long that it must sling it over its shoulder. Tokoloshes are believed to be created from dead bodies by shamans.

All cultures agree that they are malign and mischievous creatures, and they can make themselves invisible by swallowing a pebble. Despite being as small as children, they have superhuman strength and can kill oxen as well as being capable of destroying crops (or making crops poisonous). Seeing a Tokoloshe is considered to be a very bad omen – but worse still is telling another person that you have seen a Tokoloshe. This action is believed to guarantee that the Tokoloshe will return to seek a terrible retribution. So feared is the Tokoloshe by certain cultures that they raise their beds off the ground with bricks in order to remain safe from them in the night.

THE MALAIKA

The polar opposite of the Tokoloshe is the Malaika, a gentle spirit from East Africa, which can assume human form. Created from light, these spirits are transparent, and are said to sit on the shoulders of humans and whisper advice into their ears. The advice is always wise and kind. Incapable of doing evil, they are similar to the western concept of angels, and protect both human beings and heaven itself. When heaven is under attack, the Malaika throw rockets at its enemies, and these rockets are seen on earth as shooting stars. Death is a type of Malaika too, sent by god when it is time for a person's soul to ascend into heaven.

THE QUEEN OF SHEBA

The legendary Queen of Sheba (or Makeda) appears to have been based on a real life ruler of Ethiopia, who is said to have been on the throne around the 10th century BCE. She is mentioned in both the Bible and the Qur'an, and is considered by many modern day Ethiopians to be a cherished part of their heritage.

Cloven Foot

In the traditional story, Makeda makes a long pilgrimage to Jerusalem, in order to learn wisdom from King Solomon. She carries with her gifts of frankincense, myrrh and gold. Solomon has heard many tales about the queen and her mighty empire, one of which tells that the queen has a

cloven foot. He orders that his palace floor be polished until it is like glass so that when she arrives he will be able to see the reflection of her foot. As Makeda walks across the floor to greet Solomon, he catches a glimpse of her cloven foot and as soon as he does it is restored to normality.

Solomon is struck by Makeda's dark beauty, and she is dazzled by his wisdom, and the two fall in love with one another. Makeda gives birth to a son, Menelik, and founds an epic dynasty of rulers who govern Ethiopia and the land of Sheba (thought to be modern day Yemen or Ethiopia). It is claimed that it was through the union of Solomon and Makeda that Christianity first came to Africa.

ABOVE: *Queen of Sheba*, by Jean Jules Badin, circa 1870.

OTHER AFRICAN MYTHOLOGY

For Europeans, Africa was a land of mystery, intrigue and danger up until the 19th century. The largely unexplored land mass spawned countless legends – the majority of which were based either on fear and prejudice, or were inspired by the lust for adventure and riches. However, the roots of several of the legends lay in the true wonders of Africa and her people, some of which were as extraordinary as the wildest of fables to those encountering them for the first time.

AFRICAN PYGMIES

The Pygmy bush tribes of central Africa were named after the fabled Pygmaios of Greek mythology. European explorers who first encountered the tribes in the 19th century drew parallels with the myth of the Pygmaios, who were featured in the *Iliad* as a comic dwarfish people at war with a flock of cranes. The Pygmaios also attempted to bind the Greek hero Heracles as he slept. Legends of a race of diminutive people living within forests are in fact common in many mythologies, and as sailors and explorers began to encounter the indigenous tribes in Africa, myth and reality rapidly became entangled.

The real hunter-gatherer people we now refer to as Pygmies have nothing to do with the figures of Greek mythology, but no alternative term has evolved to refer to the various tribes who share a culture and belief system quite distinct from all others on the continent.

ABOVE: Mosaic depicting the river Nile landscape, from ancient Roman city of Thysdrus, Tunisia, North Africa, 3rd century CE.

THE BAMBUTI

The term Bambuti (or Mbuti) is used to refer to a group of small tribes who inhabit the Congo region. One of the oldest indigenous peoples, their hunter-gatherer lifestyles have remained more or less unchanged for centuries. Their most important god is Khonvoum, a god of hunting who carries a bow made from two intertwined snakes, which appear as a rainbow to humans. Khonvoum gathers up fragments of the stars after sunset and hurls them into the sun to revitalize it for the following day. The Bambuti believe that Khonvoum made them from red clay, with other human beings having been made from black or white clay. Some sources state that it was in fact Arebati, god of the moon, who created men by shaping clay and then pouring blood into it. Another important god to the Bambuti is Tore, god of the forest, who supplies hunters with their prey. Also a god of thunder, Tore hides in rainbows. It is believed that the Bambuti stole the secret of fire from Tore, and as a punishment he made men mortal.

After certain major events (such as a death) the Bambuti hold a ritual dance called the Molimo (named after a type of trumpet the Bambuti use to replicate the calls of animals). The dance is designed to give thanks to the forest, or to wake it from its sleep, depending on whether the event being marked was good or bad. For the Bambuti the forest is a sacred spirit, and the source of all that is good. Dances can last for several days.

VOODOO

Thanks to populist movies and tabloid newspapers, Voodoo (or Vodun) has become synonymous with witch doctors, evil curses and bloodthirsty sacrifices. No belief system has spawned more legends than Voodoo. This is largely due to Western mindsets misunderstanding the basis of the religion of Voodoo, in which spirits are believed to be capable of inhabiting countless forms, including inanimate objects. This belief remains widespread throughout many African tribes even in the present day, and whilst spirits can undoubtedly cause trouble if displeased, they can also bring great gifts to the living – something which tends to be glossed over by salacious film-makers and journalists. In Benin, Voodoo is recognized as one of the country's official religions, and it is a religion that has lasted for several hundred years.

There are numerous Voodoo gods, and they vary from region to region, but the single most important entity is Mawu, with the other entities seen as spirits working under Mawu's control. Indeed the word 'Voodoo' can be translated as 'spirit'.

In the Americas, Voodoo evolved as the slaves who left Africa attempted to cling to their beliefs in the face of brutal repression from their Christian overlords. Thus, the Voodoo of Haiti, Cuba and Brazil is a long way removed from African Vodun, and will be discussed separately (see page 101).

ABOVE: Copper West African voodoo doll.

WITCH DOCTORS

The central elements of African Voodoo are the worship of ancestors and the offering of sacrifices to the gods. These sacrifices are, in modern times, animal sacrifices – though occasionally disturbing reports of human sacrifice do emerge from remote tribal areas. Rogue witch doctors have been known to use human blood to practice a traditional form of medicine known as 'muti'. It is believed by some that killing a human being for medicine alone makes the medicine stronger, with the strongest medicine of all coming from a sacrificed child. Such practices are incredibly rare, however, and obviously highly illegal.

Since followers believe that the spirits of the dead walk freely within the same world as human beings, it is important for them to ensure that the spirits are not displeased. Spirits can also inhabit talismans (fetishes) made of wood, feather or bone, and this is the most likely source for the Voodoo doll so beloved of horror film directors.

SYMPATHETIC MAGIC

In truth, the 'poppets' that seem to have inspired the Voodoo doll legend have nothing to do with the sort of 'sympathetic magic' that might harm a person from afar. The dolls do not represent living people, but are instead figures for the spirits to inhabit. Thus the idea of sticking pins into a doll in order to cause harm to a person who is being represented by the doll makes no real sense in the Voodoo religion. Exactly where this compelling image originated from is unclear, but it is probably the result of a fusion between folk magic traditions and reports of Voodoo practices supplied by those who were unfamiliar with the Voodoo belief system.

It should be remembered that the spirits of Voodoo are capable of both good and evil, and the sort of curses that have become associated with Voodoo are relatively rare. It is more common for a follower to give thanks for rain, for example, than it is for them to ask a spirit for revenge against an enemy. That said, there is some truth in the legend of a 'Voodoo curse', with sorcerers known as Botono specializing in calling upon evil spirits to harm a particular individual or group of people.

ABOVE: Ceremonial offering of a bullock to the gods at a Vodun ceremony in the Mono region of Benin, West Africa.

VOODOO CANNIBALISM

One of the more sensational practices often associated with Voodoo is that of cannibalism. The notion came to popular attention in a book of memoirs, *Hayti* – or *The Black Republic*, written by the British diplomat Spenser St. John, published in 1884. An entire chapter of the book was devoted to the alleged widespread practice of cannibalism in Voodoo followers in Haiti, who were said to be following ancient beliefs they brought with them from their ancestral homelands in Africa. Whilst the subject of the book was Haiti, the clear implication was that cannibalism was deeply rooted in the 'dark continent' of Africa. However St. John based all of his information on hearsay, rather than any direct experience or evidence. The belief in Africa as a land of primitives was widely held at this time, and reports of cannibalism reinforced prejudices related to the superiority of Western culture over the savage African cultures.

The truth is that there is an African Voodoo ceremony that involves the eating of human flesh – but it is very rarely performed. Those who are killed by a lightning strike are believed to have angered the god of lightning (Shango) and so their corpse is roasted and tiny amounts of the flesh are eaten by the Voodoo priests who preside over the ceremony. Tales of cannibalism associated with ritual human sacrifice in Voodoo are entirely fictional, and whilst lurid tales of such behaviour do surface from time to time they have nothing to do with the bona fide religion of Voodoo.

ABOVE: Iron statue of the Vodun god, Gu, of iron and blacksmiths, covered in chicken feathers and blood which have been left as offerings.

TIMBUKTU

Like the fabled city of El Dorado (thought at one time to lie in Africa), Timbuktu was said to be a city of gold, offering the promise of fabulous wealth for anyone brave and adventurous enough to survive the journey to it through Africa's unknown heartland. Even today Timbuktu remains synonymous with an exotic faraway place: from here to Timbuktu. In reality it lies in Mali, on the southern edge of the Sahara Desert.

CITY OF GOLD

The Emperor Mansa Musa's 14th century pilgrimage to Mecca appears to have been the historical event that gave rise to the legend of Timbuktu as a city of gold. It is said that Mansa Musa gave away enormous quantities of gold on his journey, his generosity in one stop off in Cairo actually causing the Egyptian money markets to crash. Musa also used his great wealth to build mosques and a university in Timbuktu (believed to be one of the first in the world), paying the architect of the famous Djinguereber Mosque some 200kg (441 pounds) of gold for his services. Timbuktu rapidly gained a reputation as an important centre of learning for Muslim scholars, a reputation it retains to this day (the Djinguereber Mosque still stands, and is now a designated UNESCO World Heritage site).

The population boomed and merchants from across North Africa flocked to trade in its markets. Word of the fabulous wealth of Timbuktu spread, and one written account by Arab diplomat Leo Africanus proved especially effective at capturing the imagination of European adventurers. Africanus told of a city of abundance, describing the king's treasures and his vast standing army, and relating how the king paid generously for the maintenance of scholars, priests and doctors. The capture of Timbuktu by Moroccan forces in 1591, however, proved to be the beginning of the end for the city, and it was greatly in decline by the time European interest in it reached its peak in the early 19th century.

MUNGO PARK

A party of Europeans led by Scottish explorer Mungo Park set off in 1805 to chart the course of the River Niger and hopefully pinpoint the exact location of the fabled city. The expedition ended in disaster, however, with all of those involved succumbing to disease, attack or drowning. Another Scottish explorer Gordon Laing is believed to have reached Timbuktu in 1826, but he was murdered shortly after leaving the city. Two years later, disguised as an Arab, the French explorer Rene-Auguste Caillie became the first European to visit Timbuktu and live to tell the tale. He found a city made of mud-walled buildings, not gold. Caillie was perhaps not too disappointed, however – on his return to France he was able to claim a prize of 10,000 francs from the *Societe de Geographie* for being the first to discover the truth about the fabled city.

ABOVE: Rene Caillie's drawing of Timbuktu,
Mali, 1830.

PART 3

THE AMERICAS

European invasion destroyed many of the indigenous cultures of North, Central, and South America, and since the stories of the Native North Americans, Aztecs, and Incas were not written down, much has been lost to us. What remains, however, is truly dazzling.

From the Inuit of the Arctic circle down to the desert regions of the Navajo, North America is a treasury of diverse cultures and correspondingly diverse mythologies. Thankfully, many of the indigenous tribes of Native America survived the turmoil of conflict and invasion. The fierce determination of these tribes to preserve the cultures of their ancestors through stories and songs has saved some of the most beautiful of the world's myths from oblivion.

In South and Central America, the myths and legends passed down to us are largely filtered through the minds of the conquering Europeans, though a precious selection of original gods and spirits have survived through traditions of oral storytelling and through monuments, statues, and other artefacts. These give us a glimpse of a world of awesome supernatural forces and vast – often bloodthirsty – rituals.

NATIVE NORTH AMERICAN MYTHOLOGY

The disparate tribes of North America share a common belief in a 'Great Spirit' and the sanctity of the natural world. The seasons, the elements, and man's connection with the animals and the spirits are common themes. Stories were often shared at tribal gatherings with dances, trances, and songs all forming part of the sacred rituals enacted to give thanks and to keep ancestors content.

APACHE

The world, according to an Apache creation myth, was formed from a small ball that the Creator made from the sweat of the first four gods. The myth begins with the gods kicking the ball around until it grows in size, and the wind climbs inside the ball to inflate it. The trickster, Tarantula, then spins a thread which it attaches to the ball, and it pulls on the thread in each direction until the ball is the size of the earth. The Creator then makes all of the features of the world and populates it with human beings and animals.

CHEROKEE

The Cherokee tell of a time before the earth, when all of the animals lived in an overcrowded sky above a vast ocean. The water beetle explored the ocean and brought mud from the depths to create land. A buzzard then flew across the watery mud, and every time its wings hit the water a mountain was created.

LAKOTA

The Lakota tell of how time was created by a rift in the heavens between the sun god and his wife, the moon. The rift was said to have been caused by the trickster spider, Iktomi. The gods of the four winds were scattered to create space. Iktomi then travelled to the underworld, where human beings used to live, and he tricked them into coming to the surface before sealing the return route. Human beings thought they were travelling to paradise but instead found the earth full of suffering and hardship.

NAVAJO

The Navajo believe that human beings were created from insect people who fought one another in three lower worlds before finally learning to live with one another in the fourth world. The different genders of man and women were created from human beings who did not recognize the importance of one another's contributions. The stories relating to the first humans are set in the area known as Dinetah, the traditional spiritual homeland of the Navajo, which once encompassed parts of what are now New Mexico, Colorado, Utah, and Arizona. The boundaries of Dinetah were marked by four holy mountains, and the Holy People instructed the Navajo never to leave the area of land marked out by these mountains.

SEMINOLE

For the Seminole, the Creator made all of the animals and placed them in a shell on top of a mountain. He told them that when the time was right the shell would crack open and they could all emerge to take their proper place in the world. In time, the roots of a nearby tree encircled the shell and caused it to crack out, and the first to emerge was the panther, followed by the bird, and then all of the other animals. A similar tale is told by the Haida, though in their version a raven pecks at a clam to release the male animals. The female animals were released separately.

ABOVE: Apache leader, Geronimo (1820-1909).
Photograph by Aaron Canady, circa 1907.

SCARFACE

The story of the brave warrior Scarface is told (in two or three slightly different forms) by Algonquin/Blackfoot tribes. The eponymous Scarface (or Poia) is usually said to have got his scar whilst battling and killing a bear, which scratched him with its mighty claw. The scar so disfigured him that no woman could bear to look at him, and so despite his great skills at hunting he was unable to find a wife.

DANGEROUS JOURNEY

Scarface falls in love with the chief's daughter, but she has pledged to the sun god that she would never marry. She tells Scarface that she will marry him if he can persuade the sun god to release her from her promise, and return from the sun god without the scar on his face. Scarface sets out on the long and dangerous journey to find the sun god, and overcomes many obstacles to reach his destination. He meets Apsirahts, the son of the sun god, and Apsirahts pledges to take him up to his father's lodge at the top of a mountain.

While Scarface and Apsirahts are out hunting, Apsirahts is attacked by ferocious birds and his life is only saved when Scarface kills the birds. Upon learning that Scarface has saved his son, the sun god grants Scarface his wish to marry the chief's daughter, and removes the scar that disfigures his face. Scarface returns to his village as a handsome warrior, and only the chief's daughter recognizes him. The two are married, and Scarface is forever after known as Smoothface.

MORNING STAR

In another version of the story, Scarface's mother falls in love with Morning Star and is taken up to the skies to live with him. However, she disobeys his order never to move the cooking pot (or in some versions a giant turnip) that blocks the hole through which she ascended, and so she and Scarface are banished back to earth. In this version of the story, Scarface received his scar when the leather cord they were lowered to earth on rubbed against his cheek. Scarface grows up and seeks out his father (who in some versions resides in the stars, rather than being the sun god) in order to gain the hand of his beloved. Knowing that his mother has been banished from the sky-country forever, he is at a loss to work out how to return to his homeland until he sees the rays of the sun reflected in the Pacific Ocean. The reflection forms a path to the sun which Scarface follows. Finding Scarface asleep on his doorstep, the sun is about to kill the mortal when the moon intercedes, recognizing the scar on his face. The happy ending remains the same, as Scarface is granted his wish to have the scar removed, and returns to Earth to marry his beloved.

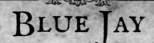

BLUE JAY

Many Native American tribes have stories about the trickster spirit Blue Jay, who can change from the shape of a man to that of a bird at will. Blue Jay is often challenged to contests or trials, and he generally manages to win through, with a little bit of cheating or trickery. For example, when challenged to a diving contest he wins by coming up for air under a bed of reeds, whilst his opponent attempts to dive using a single lungful of air. A contest to see who can climb a pinnacle of ice is won by Blue Jay after he uses his wings to fly upwards rather than climb. His trickery does not always succeed, however, and several of the stories end with the death of Blue Jay. The stories are frequently comic in tone and the numerous deaths of Blue Jay never really mark the real end of the trickster god.

UP TO MISCHIEF

One story gives a good indication of Blue Jay's mischievous spirit. Blue Jay's elder sister Ioi (who features in many of his tales) dies and is taken to the spirit world. Blue Jay visits her there and finds her surrounded by piles of skeletons. She tells him that the skeletons reassemble themselves when no one is around, and walk around like the living. However, whenever they are startled they collapse into piles of bones again. On learning this, Blue Jay waits until the skeletons reassemble themselves then joins them on a fishing trip (in moss-covered canoes full of holes). To amuse himself, he deliberately sings loudly to startle them, and roars with laughter as they collapse into heaps of bones.

ANGRY BONES

One night he mixes up the piles of bones so that the next time they reassemble themselves their body parts are mismatched. The skeleton of a child cannot stand because Blue Jay has placed the head of an old man on its body. The old man, meanwhile, has the head of a child and feels light-headed. The next night Blue Jay switches around everybody's legs, so that children have the legs of adults, the men have the legs of women and vice versa. Needless to say, the ghostly skeletons become annoyed at Blue Jay's games and he is forced to leave the spirit world.

His sister Ioi gives Blue Jay five buckets of water before he leaves, to help him pass the burning prairies. She warns him not to pour the water out until he comes to the fourth burning prairie, but Blue Jay empties the buckets fighting earlier fires and by the time he reaches the fourth burning prairie he has no water left. Blue Jay is killed by the fire, and returns to the spirit world. This time the canoes look in pristine condition to him, because, Ioi explains, things look different to the dead.

GLUSKAP

Another trickster god who features in many Native American myths is Gluskap (or Glooscap), who was a particular favourite of the Algonquin. Gluskap was a divine being who came from the East, though he had the form of a man. He taught the Indians all that they know – everything from the names of the stars to how to hunt and fish – and is portrayed in most stories as a wise and grave character. Some myths state that he created human beings from his mother's body, and that his brother Malsum was responsible for creating all the things that annoyed or threatened human beings. Gluskap is thus seen as the protector of humankind, while his brother Malsum is constantly trying to harm people. Like King Arthur in Celtic legends, some say that Gluskap will return to help his people when they are most in need.

MYSTERIOUS PARCEL

Though Gluskap tends to look favourably on requests for help, there is often a sting in the tale for those who do not follow his instructions. One story, for example, relates how a young man goes to Gluskap asking for help in finding a wife. The man is ugly, and has been shunned by hundreds of women whom he asked to be his wife. Gluskap gives him a small parcel, with instructions not to open the parcel until he gets home. Though the man's friends beg him not to open it on the way home, curiosity gets the better of the man. As soon as he undoes the parcel, hundreds of beautiful young women fly out in all directions and bury the man beneath their weight. His cries for help grow fainter and fainter as he is crushed into the earth. The next morning all the women have

ABOVE: Ancient Puebloan (Anasazi) pictographs including the trickster god of fertility represented by the flute player on his back. Canyon de Chelly, Arizona, USA.

vanished and all that is left of the young man is the scattered powder of his crushed bones.

Gluskap has also been known to turn those who ask him for immortality into rocks or trees, though in general he is a benevolent deity who will grant most reasonable requests.

OWL'S FEATHER

One story relates that Gluskap's brother Malsum killed him with the feather of an owl – the only thing that could harm Gluskap. However, he returned from the dead and managed to slay his brother, who then changed into an evil wolf, Lox. Malsum's followers tried to avenge him by attacking Gluskap, but after numerous battles Gluskap finally prevailed. He held a celebratory feast for all of the animals by the shores of a lake, and then sailed off in a canoe. The animals, who had previously all spoken the same language, discovered that each species spoke a different language once he had gone.

Gluskap is sometimes portrayed as a rabbit, though it is said he can take on whichever shape he wants.

NAPI

Variations of the trickster figure are found in the myths of many Native American tribes, with perhaps the most famous being the Old Man or Napi.

Whilst the Old Man Napi (or Napa) sometimes has godlike powers, he is more often portrayed as all too human, and his countless deceptions and acts of dishonesty are almost always discovered and punished. For example, in one story Napi decides to steal a pair of leggings from the sun god. The leggings are the sun's prized possession, made from coloured porcupine quills, and he wears them every day before taking them off and using them as a pillow at night.

Napi sneaks into the sun god's home while he is sleeping, but is constantly being startled by noises which scare him and force him to flee. One night, however, he does finally manage to steal the leggings, and he makes good his escape. Tired from his exertions, he falls asleep, and when he wakes he finds the sun standing over him and laughing at him. The terrified Napi runs off and the sun reclaims his leggings.

TRYING TO TRICK THE SUN GOD

Napi tries to steal the leggings a second time, with much the same results. This time, however, the sun god is cross with Napi and warns him that if he ever attempts to steal them again, the sun will use his mighty power to harm him. He reminds Napi that nobody can hide from the sun, no matter how fast they run. Realizing this, Napi gives up and pledges to leave the sun alone.

Like Gluskap, Napi is sometimes paired with a brother, who generally causes harm. One story suggests that Napi's brother made the white races, and Napi made the Native American races. Another suggests that Napi and his brother are the sons of the sun god and the moon. The moon is a female who chases her husband around the sky after he chopped off her head in revenge for her making love to a rattlesnake.

COYOTE

In many Native American cultures, Coyote is credited with bringing humanity the gift of fire, and in some belief systems he also invented copulation. Perhaps his most famous incarnation, however, is in the Nez Perce tribe's story of Coyote and The Shadow People, where Coyote's actions lead to humankind being forever separated from the spirit realm of the dead.

When Coyote's wife dies, a spirit appears and asks Coyote if he would like to see her again in the underworld. Coyote replies enthusiastically that he would, and he agrees to the spirit's demand that he must do exactly as the spirit tells him. The spirit leads Coyote to a lodge where the dead appear as shadows whenever darkness falls.

DON'T LOOK BACK

After staying at the lodge for several days, and meeting many of his departed friends, Coyote is told that he can leave with his wife and return to the land of the living. However, the spirit tells him he must not touch his wife until they have crossed five mountains. Coyote follows this advice until the last night of their journey, when his wife's shadowy form changes and he can see her clearly. He rushes to embrace her and she disappears back into the spirit realm forever. As seen in the European section, the story of Coyote has similarities with that of Orpheus (see page 21).

ABOVE: Petroglyphs of Anasazi of unknown origin on a boulder overlooking Salt River Canyon in the San Carlos Apache Reservation, Arizona, USA.

CHANGING WOMAN AND OTHER FEMALE SPIRITS

The Apache and Navajo believe that Changing Woman is one of the most important goddesses. She is able to change her age, from a baby to an old woman, by walking across the horizon. When she grows old she grows lonely, so she made human beings to keep her company.

Sometimes she is described as being the same as Turquoise Woman, though in other accounts Turquoise Woman and White Shell Woman were created by Changing Woman from the flakes of her own dry skin. The different names may represent the different colours of her clothes as the seasons change.

COPPPER WOMAN

Copper Woman is another lonely spirit, who brought a crab shell to life with her tears. The half-human and half-crab creature lives in the sea during the day but returns to Copper Woman each night. He makes love to her, never speaking, but keeping her from ever feeling lonely.

CORN WOMAN

Corn Woman, sometimes Corn Mother or Selu, is responsible for providing human beings with corn – though accounts of how she produces the corn differ from region to region. The most widely held belief is that she once lived side by side with humans, and gave them delicious corn meals every day. Curious to find out where the corn came from, the human beings spy on her and observe her scraping sores and boils from her body into a pot. Disgusted, they then refuse to eat her corn. In response she instructs the humans to sow her dead skin in the ground, and corn sprouts from that day forth. This is said to be how human beings came to learn how to farm the land.

STAR MAIDEN

Star Maiden was said to come to Earth with her sisters, descending from the sky each night to dance in a circle. She is observed by a human hunter who falls in love with her. Knowing that he will scare off the star fairies if he approaches them, he changes himself into a mouse and creeps up on them as they dance. Suddenly transforming himself back into a human again, he grabs Star Maiden and she cannot escape with her sisters back into the sky. She soon falls in love with the hunter, however, and they have a child.

After some years Star Maiden goes back to the sky with her child, as she misses her home. Her child grows up to become a man and asks Star Maiden if he can visit his father back on earth. Her son thus descends back to Earth in a basket and invites his father to come and live with them in the sky. His father agrees, and brings with him gifts which he has taken from various animals such as a feather from an eagle and the cast-off skin of a snake. The gods in the stars are so delighted with the gifts that each becomes one of the animals, and they can now be seen in their animal shapes in the constellations.

ABOVE: Navajo indian dressed up as goddess
Haschebaad, photograph by Edward S. Curtis,
1904.

OTHER NORTH AMERICAN & CARIBBEAN MYTHS & LEGENDS

INUIT MYTHOLOGY

Many Inuit cultures believe the world was created by a raven – sometimes with his wife's help. The harsh environment of the Inuit led to them living in fear of cruel unseen forces, and many monsters lurk in the snowy wastes of their world, and in the dark depths of their oceans.

KIVIUQ

The central figure in Inuit stories is the great shaman wanderer Kiviuq, who has lived for many centuries (or lived many lives, depending on the storyteller). Stories of Kiviuq's journeys are legion, found in numerous different Inuit cultures across Canada, Alaska and Greenland, some of whom render his name as Qayaq or Qooqa. He travels on foot, by sled, by kayak, and even on the backs of giant fishes, and it is said that he will return to visit his people one last time before he dies.

In many of the stories told about Kiviuq he overcomes some seemingly impossible obstacle, often using his magical powers, in order to continue his wanderings. He does battle with half-fish, half-human creatures, narrowly avoids being sliced in two by the Big Bee Woman and briefly marries a beautiful wolf-woman. The relationship ends when the wolf-woman's jealous mother kills and skins her daughter. The mother then wears her daughter's skin to try and convince Kiviuq that she is his wife.

KIVIUQ'S KINDNESS

The most widely told story illustrates Kiviuq's kindness and non-judgemental character. Kiviuq befriends the grandson of an old woman, a boy that everybody else makes fun of because he is an orphan. After the boy's coat is torn by his tormentors, his grandmother makes him a new one made from seal skin found on the beach. She tells him to return to face the bullies and pretend to be a seal. When he does this, the men of the village chase him into the sea, pursuing him in kayaks. The old woman then causes a terrible storm to descend upon the men and drown them all. Only Kiviuq and the boy survive.

In some versions of the story, Kiviuq is himself the young orphaned boy in question, and he takes revenge against the men not only for bullying him but for murdering his father. Kiviuq's father is said to have been half-man and half-seal – a Tuutalik – and during one especially bad winter he helped the man to find the breathing holes of seals in the ice. He swam through one hole in order to call the seals for the hunters, but one of the hunters harpooned him instead.

In another version, Kiviuq's brothers were all killed and so he was given magical amulets by his father to protect him. In this version Kiviuq returns home from his adventures to find his parents dead, and his grief is so great that he turns into a hawk and flies away from the world forever.

SEDNA

Sedna was said to be so hungry that she ate everything in her family's home, and then began eating the family itself. Her father, waking to discover that he has lost an arm to her voracious appetite, throws her into the ocean (presumably one-handed). Sedna attempts to cling onto the side of her father's kayak, and so her father cuts off her fingers, sending her down to the bottom of the ocean. There, she becomes goddess of all the sea creatures, which have grown from her severed fingers.

In many versions of her story she is married to a dog, having found no man good enough for her. It is this marriage, some say, that caused her father to throw her into the sea. Others state that she was taken from a kayak by a sea-bird or bird-man, rather than thrown into the sea by her father. One version states that Sedna was seduced by a seabird who treated her badly, and that her father tried to rescue her but hundreds of seabirds surrounded his kayak so he threw his daughter into the sea to appease them. The father in question is sometimes named as Anguta, the Inuit creator god. All seem to agree that Sedna ended up in the oceans, and that her fingers were cut off, and that all the sea creatures grew from these fingers. Most stories tell that Sedna grew a fish's tail.

GODDESS OF THE SEA CREATURES

As goddess of sea creatures, Sedna was vital to the Inuit's food supply, and so she was a very important deity. When angry, she could lock all the sea creatures in ice and thus cause the Inuit to starve. In addition, Sedna was believed to live in, and rule over, the Inuit underworld, Adlivun.

ADLIVUN AND QUIDLIVUN

Adlivun is the name the Inuit give to both their underworld and to the name of the souls of the departed. The underworld is believed to exist beneath the land and the sea, and is usually referred to as a frozen wasteland. The dead who reside there are kept for a period of one year by Sedna while their souls are purified before the trip to the paradise of Quidlivun, the Land of the Moon. Once the dead reach Quidlivun they rest in eternal peace. Only those who have lived pure lives reach Quidlivun, the rest are reincarnated on earth.

The dead are ferried from the earth to Adlivun by Pinga, the goddess of the hunt, and Sedna's father, Anguta. When an Inuit dies he or she is wrapped in caribou skin and buried. After three days of mourning, the friends and relatives of the deceased return to the grave and ritualistically circle it three times, then offer venison to the spirit of the deceased.

ABOVE: Digital illustration of Inuit goddess, Sedna, depicted as a walrus with animal gripping head.

THE SASQUATCH

The belief in a species of giant ape-like men occurs in many different localities, but perhaps the most famous example in modern times is the legend of Bigfoot, which grew in turn from alleged sightings of a Sasquatch in the Canadian province of British Columbia. First Nation Canadians had long spoken of a fearsome breed of ape-like creatures in the northwest Pacific region, and the artist Paul Kane recorded that he could not persuade any of the indigenous population to act as his guide when seeking to visit Mount Saint Helens in 1847, as they feared the skoocums who inhabited the mountains of that area.

News reporter J. W. Burns wrote a series of articles about the local legend for a Canadian newspaper in the 1920s, and is credited with first using the word Sasquatch to describe the creature, taking the name from the Halkomelem language of the indigenous culture.

RUBY CREEK INCIDENT

In 1941 the Sasquatch was said to have terrorized a family in what was to become known as the Ruby Creek Incident. A mother fled from her home with her children after a 2.4m (8 foot) tall ape walking on its hind legs came out of the woods and headed towards them.

The legend came to the world's attention again in 1973 after a Canadian conservation officer discovered a 53cm (21 inch) footprint which appeared to belong to an ape that walked on two legs. Further footprints were found over the course of the next decade at Lake Berriere and Manitoba – the credibility of the latter report receiving a boost due to the fact that its discoverer was a member of the Royal Canadian Mounted Police.

The legend of Bigfoot, a similar ape-man figure said to be living in the woods at Bluff Creek California, is thought to have been inspired by the Sasquatch stories. Now widely considered to have been a hoax perpetrated by local logger Ray Wallace, the legend made global headlines in 1958 when not only were footprints found but Bigfoot appeared to have been captured on video tape. Wallace's family confessed to the hoax after his death, but believers maintain he could not have been responsible for all of the sightings reported.

THE YETI

The Yeti or Abominable Snowman is a closely related legend relating to an ape-like figure living in the Himalayan region of Nepal and Tibet. A short piece of film that appeared to prove the existence of the Yeti (the so-called Snow Walker film) was also later revealed to be a hoax.

Countless curious footprints purporting to belong to ape-men have been found in remote locations across the world, but to date no incontrovertible evidence has emerged to prove the existence of such a species. Sceptics have pointed out that such a large animal would require a plentiful food supply and would thus be obliged to hunt frequently, making it highly unlikely that they would have been able to avoid detection by humans in the 21st century.

ABOVE: A frame from a cine film of Bigfoot, taken by Roger Patterson, 20 October 1967, at Bluff Creek, Northern California, USA.

THE MEXICAN DAY OF THE DEAD

In Mexico it is believed that the dead can return to communicate with the living on The Day of the Dead, *El Dia de Los Muertos*, November 1–2. Friends and relatives of the dead bring flowers (marigolds being a popular choice) and skulls made of sugar to graveyards to try and attract the departed, and they share stories and anecdotes about the deceased. Sometimes confused with Halloween, The Day of the Dead is actually more about celebrating the lives of those who have departed rather than the supernatural hauntings that characterize Halloween. Toys are brought for dead children, with tequila and other beverages being common offerings for the adults. Some families build shrines in their homes, often adorned with Christian symbols, and altars are also constructed in public buildings with ofrendas, or offerings, placed upon them.

Catrina figurines are also a common sight, depicting rich and fashionable women wearing ornate hats with their skeletons clearly visible beneath their clothes. They symbolize the fact that death comes to everyone, regardless of their social status. The festival is thought to have its origins in an Aztec festival dedicated to the goddess Mictecacihuatl, the Lady of the Dead who watched over the bones of the deceased in the underworld. Similar festivals are held at about the same time of the year in Brazil and Spain, and several Asian and African countries also have festivals which specifically celebrate the dead.

ABOVE LEFT: Lithograph showing a skeletal couple by Mexican illustrator Jose Guadalupe Posada. Since his death, his work has become associated with the Mexican festival, Dia de los Muertos.

ABOVE RIGHT: Skull candy sold during the Dia de los Muertos festival.

CARIBBEAN MYTHS AND LEGENDS

The world was created by the spider god Anansi, according to a myth prevalent in the West Indies. This myth is believed to have originated in Ghana, though the trickster nature of Anansi is also a key feature of many spirits in Native American stories. Most of Anansi's tricks backfire upon him, and many of the stories appear to be entirely for entertainment rather than containing spiritual significance.

THE DUPPY

In Jamaica it is believed that a type of spirit called a Duppy can escape from the coffin of a recently deceased person if proper care is not taken. It is believed the body has two separate souls – one that goes to heaven to be judged and another earthly soul, which can become a Duppy and haunt the living at night. The belief arose in West Africa and has parallels with Voodoo spirits and zombies.

THE MONEY MOTH

Across the Caribbean the Black Witch moth is believed to be a portent of bad luck, and this is especially true in Jamaica where it is known as The Duppy Bat. The moth appears in many legends and folk tales of the Caribbean. In the Bahamas, however, under the guise of The Money Moth it is associated with good luck and it is believed that anyone the moth lands on will come into money.

THE DOUEN

The Douen of Trinidad and Tobago are representations of the souls of dead children who were not baptized. Their feet face backwards, they wear floppy straw hats and they are neither male nor female. Floppy hats aside, they wear no clothes, and never grow to more than 60cm (two foot) tall. The Douen are believed to play pranks on the living, and attempt to entice other unbaptized children away to join them in the forest. Parents believe that they should never use their child's name when they call to their children in case the Douen, having learned the child's name, use it to call the child into the forest. The Douen are particularly active when the moon is full, and can sometimes be heard outside houses, whimpering for their mothers. They do also have a kinder side, as they are said to help wounded animals by imitating their calls in order to confuse pursuing hunters.

THE LUSCA

As may be expected in an area of small islands surrounded by oceans, mythical sea creatures abound in Caribbean legends. One of the most famous, the Lusca, is a type of giant octopus that can change colour and which is capable of dragging men to a watery grave. It is believed to lurk off the coast of the Bahamas and grow to a size of 25 metres (75 feet) – though no specimens of this size have ever been found. Other accounts suggest that the Lusca is half-octopus and half-shark, or a multi-headed sea-dragon.

CARIBBEAN VOODOO

Most commonly associated with Haiti, Caribbean Voodoo has its roots in the Vodun of Africa, but evolved into a distinct belief system after being brought to North and Central America by displaced slaves, where it was shaped by the prevailing Christian religion. The creator Bondye equates to the supreme God of Christian belief, with the lesser spirits called Loa equating with saints. The Loa are seen as having more to do with the day-to-day lives of humans, and so it is to these spirits that Voodoo practices are directed.

One of the most important spirits is Papa Legba, who speaks all languages and acts as an intermediary between the human world and the Loa. Rituals begin and end by invoking Papa Legba, as without him contact with the Loa is impossible. He is often portrayed as walking with a crutch or cane, wearing a wide-brimmed hat and smoking a pipe or cigarette, and he often has a dog in tow. His cane represents the spine that supports the world, and his modest dress is indicative of the humble nature which belies his great power. Gifts and offerings to Papa Legba are usually modest, for his needs are simple.

SPIRITS OF LOVE

Appeals to the Erzulie (or Ezili) family of spirits are common, as they are the spirits of love. The most important is Erzulie Freda, who wears three wedding rings to symbolize her marriages to the serpent spirit Damballa, the sea spirit Agwe and the warrior spirit Ogoun. She is generous yet fickle, capable of giving love but also of sending infidelity to torment humanity.

At Voodoo ceremonies, the spirits take possession of participants and speak through them, usually as they dance and sing. The ceremonies are presided over by a high priest – the Houngan, or priestess – the Mambo.

BLACK MAGIC

The association of Voodoo with black magic, or Hoodoo, and Satanism is largely fictitious, though there is a belief that certain Voodoo sorcerers can create zombies and place curses on individuals. Such practices tend to occur in remote rural areas and are not a feature of orthodox Voodoo. The myth of Voodoo zombies who can be controlled and forced to perform their master's will was popularized by Ian Fleming in the James Bond story *Live and Let Die*. The association between Voodoo and Satanism is a similarly artificial modern construct. Satan is very rarely evoked in Voodoo, and the association between the two stems largely from horror films and folksongs from the Mississippi Delta.

It is said that in 1791, at Bois Caiman in Haiti, a Voodoo ceremony took place in which Haitians attempted to rid themselves of French rule, though this has been disputed by some experts who claim the ceremony is legend rather than fact. Slaves were said to have gathered in the woods and pledged to kill all of their white oppressors during the secret ceremony. A week later a violent insurrection by the Haitians left 1,000 French men, women and children dead but was ultimately, brutally, crushed. Haiti finally achieved independence in 1804.

LEFT: Mural in the Hamel street neighbourhood of Havana, Cuba, painted by Salvador Gonzalez. The street has become a temple for worshippers of the Vodun and Yoruba religions.

MESOAMERICAN MYTHOLOGY

The pre-Columbian societies of Central America flourished before the arrival of the Spanish in the 15th and 16th centuries, and the mighty empires of the Aztecs and the Maya produced many compelling, bloodythirsty myths. The empires were also the subjects of many myths that outsiders wove, including tales of fabulous wealth and a belief in fate so absolute that it ultimately destroyed the cultures.

MAYAN MYTHOLOGY

The *Popl Vuh* or *Book of Council*, dating from the 16th century and found in the Guatemalan highlands provides the bulk of the available source material for Mayan myths, though the *Chilam Balam* books from the Yucatan also give valuable insights into this ancient culture's belief system. The latter appears to prophesy the coming of the Spanish invaders who were to conquer and all but obliterate the mighty Mayan Empire.

MAYAN CREATION MYTH

At first there was only 'the calm sea and the great expanse of the sky'. The feathered serpent god Gukumatz and other gods including the god of storms and fire, Huracan, meet to form a council of gods and agree that when dawn breaks man should appear on earth. They create the earth simply by saying the word earth.

They then embark on three failed attempts to create a being – humankind – that can worship them. Firstly, they create all of the animals in the world, but they have no language to give praise to their creators, and so the gods decree that they will serve humans.

FIRST ATTEMPT

Next they create men from the earth's mud, but these talk senselessly and crumble too easily, and so they are destroyed. They then create men from wood, but these lack reason, intellect and memory. They walk but have no blood or sweat, and accomplish nothing. The gods send a terrible flood (akin to the floods mentioned in Genesis and Gilgamesh but here a flood of burning resin) to sweep away all the wooden mannequins. The wooden men retreat to the forests, and the Maya believed monkeys to be the remnants of this experiment in human design.

Finally the gods succeed in making the first true men and later, women, from corn and their own blood. It is blood that unites men and the gods in the Mayan belief system, and the Mayans were thus careful to include blood in their offerings and rituals.

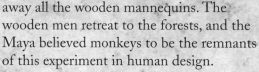

ABOVE: Statue of Quetzalcoatl the serpent god of Central America.

THE MAYA HERO TWINS

The twin boys Xbalanque and Hunahpu were the sons of Hun Hanahpu, who some scholars equate with a Mayan corn god, and like their father they were skilled ball players (the Maya often used a ball game called tlachtli to settle differences without resorting to warfare). Hun Hanahpu was summoned to Xibalba – the underworld – and killed by the Lords of the Underworld. In some versions of the story, Hun Hanahpu lost his ball down the hole that leads to Xibalba and was killed after the lords challenged him to a game of tlachtli that he subsequently lost. In other versions the noise of Hun Hanahpu and his brother playing tlachtli disturbed the Lords of the Underworld and they challenged the brothers to play on their tlachtli court in the underworld. The Lords used a ball of blades and the brothers were decapitated.

SPITTING SKULL

Hun Hanahpu's skull was then hung in a tree, and when one of the daughters of a Lord of the Underworld ('Xquic') approached this tree the skull spat on her hand, making her pregnant with the twin boys. After their birth, Xquic gave the boys to Hun Hanahpu's mother, who raised them in the upper world. When they grew older, they learned of their father's fate (after torturing the story out of a talking rat) and decided to avenge their father. The twins thus embark on a journey through the underworld in a motif that recurs in the myths of many cultures.

Xbalanque takes the lead role in the story that follows, as the brothers are tested by the lords of Xibalba and finally manage to triumph. Each time the twins play a game of tlachtli against the Lords they win, and are punished by having to spend the night in one of the many torture houses that Xibalba has to offer. They survive the ordeals of the House of Lances, the House of Ice, House of Tigers, House of Fire and House of Bats – though Hanahpu is decapitated and has to be restored back to life by a magical turtle.

FINAL VICTORY

They achieve final victory over the Lords of Xibalba with the help of the sorcerers Bacam and Xulu. The twins claim to be able to restore the dead back to life, and when challenged to prove their claims kill and resurrect both the Hound of Death and themselves, to the astonishment of the Lords of the Underworld. The story suggests that this was either enough to make the Lords subservient, or that in trying to emulate the feat of the brothers the Lords killed themselves. Either way, the twins defeat death and they return to the upper world in triumph. They are then sent to the heavens where they are transformed into the sun and the sky.

In the story outlined in the *Popul Vuh*, the twins have many battles before they even reach the underworld – including killing a bird-demon and his sons, and conquering their two half-brothers, Hun Chowen and Hun Batz, who planned to assassinate them. These they are said to have turned into howler monkeys, which were believed by the Maya to be the gods of scribes. Images of these events have been found depicted on Mayan ceramics which predate any written texts that have survived, suggesting that the stories collected in *Popul Vuh* were already very ancient by the time they were set down in writing.

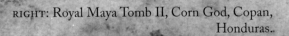

RIGHT: Royal Maya Tomb II, Corn God, Copan, Honduras.

Aztec Mythology

The Aztecs arrived at their home in what is now Mexico City as the result of a prophesy. The story tells of how the Aztecs journeyed south until they saw an eagle perched in a cactus tree (commonly the eagle is described as eating a snake, but there is no mention of the snake in the original texts). Having been foretold that this sight would greet them at their new home, the Aztecs began to build their capital, Tenochtitlan, in the middle of an artificial island.

Aztec Creation Myths

The Aztecs had several creation myths, but the central story is of five suns - the Earth Sun, the Wind Sun, the Rain Sun, the Water Sun and the Earthquake Sun. The last of these related to the world in which the Aztecs lived – the other suns, or attempts at creation, all failed. The humble god Nanhuatzin (or Nanauatl, whose name means 'full of sores') and the proud god Tecuciztecatl vied for the honour of sacrificing themselves to form the sun. Nanhuatzin jumped into the fire that the gods had created, after Tecuciztecatl became afraid, but Tecuciztecatl jumped in afterwards and so two suns were initially created. The gods decided this made the sky too bright and so a rabbit was thrown into the face of Tecuciztecatl and he became the moon. Nanhuatzin grew tired very easily and so the gods sacrificed their own blood to ensure that he had the energy to travel across the sky.

The Five Suns

The sun was absolutely central to Aztec mythology, and each of the five suns (or ages) of creation had its own god or goddess. In addition there was another sun god who was perhaps even more important – Huitzilopochtli, the god of war, who fought on behalf of the sun to ensure that it could move across the sky. Without Huitzilopochtli's power it was believed the sun would stand still or fall from the heavens. The Aztecs regarded themselves as 'the people of the sun'. They believed that they were living in the time of the fifth sun, the Earthquake Sun, and that this world would end with a series of massive earthquakes.

Created from a Crocodile

A second creation myth tells that the world was created by the twin gods Tezcatlipoca and Quetzalcoatl. The universe contained nothing but a vast ocean ruled by the terrible crocodile-like creature Cipactli, which had a jaw at every joint in its body. Whenever Tezcatlipoca and Quetzalcoatl created anything it would fall into the ocean and be eaten by Cipactli.

Tezcatlipoca uses his foot as bait to lure Cipactli, and when she bites on it he and his brother grab hold of her and tear her body into pieces, which they use to create the world. The heavens are made from Cipactli's head, the world from her middle and the underworld from her tail.

Other parts of Cipactli are used to create human beings, and it was believed that humans had to offer their blood to Cipactli as compensation for her pains. Tezcatlipoca is depicted with only one foot, having lost the one he used to lure Cipactli, and he and his brother feature in many other Aztec tales.

RIGHT: Close-up of the centre of the 20-ton Aztec Sun Stone – discovered in 1790 in Mexico. City.

TEZCATLIPOCA AND QUETZALCOATL

Not withstanding the fact that one account claims they created the world together, the brother gods Tezcatlipoca (depicted as a jaguar) and Quetzalcoatl (depicted as a serpent) are sworn enemies in Aztec myth. The story of the five suns tells that Tezcatlipoca ruled as the first sun god, but was struck down by his brother Quetzalcoatl, who then ruled in his place. Later Tezcatlipoca returns to strike down Quetzalcoatl. The brothers appear to symbolize creation through conflict.

Quetzalcoatl is associated in Aztec myth with the wind, dawn, arts and crafts, and knowledge. Tezcatlipoca is associated with night, hurricanes, obsidian, and sorcery. Each was of great importance to the Aztecs, and each had a thirst for blood which they believed could only be satiated by sacrifice.

In one tale Tezcatlipoca tricks Quetzalcoatl into getting drunk and committing an act of incest with his sister (though in other versions Tezcatlipoca shows his own monstrous reflection to Quetzalcoatl who, believing it to be his reflection rather than his brother's, becomes disgusted with himself and full of self-hate). Quetzalcoatl goes into exile, ascending into heaven as the Morning Star, or carried off to sea on a raft drawn by serpents (depending on which version of the story you read). It was believed by the Aztecs that Quetzalcoatl would return – leading to the later legend that they mistook the Spanish invader Cortes for Quetzalcoatl returning in a new form.

ABOVE: Quetzalcoatl, the Toltec and Aztec god.

HUMAN SACRIFICE IN AZTEC CULTURE

Whilst reports of human sacrifice were quite possibly exaggerated by Spanish conquistadors, we do know that the ritual murder of human beings did take place across Mesoamerica, and was especially common in Aztec ceremonies. Archaeological evidence from the Great Pyramid of Tenochtitlan and other Aztec sites suggests that not only was human sacrifice fact rather than legend, it may have gone hand-in-hand with cannibalism on some occasions.

It is thought that the Aztecs held ceremonies involving human sacrifice every 20 days or so (once a month in the Aztec's 18 month a year calendar). The first sacrifice ever recorded was that of King Coxcox's daughter, who was sacrificed and skinned during the creation of Tenochtitlan. Sacrifices were believed to be necessary in order to pay a debt of blood to the gods, who had sacrificed themselves in order to create the world for man. A particularly important ceremony called the New Fire Ceremony took place every 52 years, for it was believed that if the gods were not strong enough then the sun would fall after this period of time. A sacrificed body was burnt and the fire was taken to all of the homes in the neighbourhood.

REMOVING THE HEART

During sacrifice the heart of the victim was usually cut out with a sacrificial knife made from obsidian or flint, and offered to the gods whilst still beating. The Aztecs believed that the heart contained the soul of the person, and also a fragment of the heat of the sun. Sometimes the sacrifice was flayed, burned, shot with arrows, or killed in gladiatorial combat, depending on which ceremony was being held to honour which god. Those who sacrificed themselves were believed to go straight to the second-highest heaven (the very highest heaven was reserved for those who died as innocents in infancy).

Many of those sacrificed were captured enemies or slaves. The warrior responsible for capturing an enemy who was later sacrificed was given the body of the enemy after the ceremony. The warrior then ate parts of the body, and ascended one more rung in the Aztec social ladder, which rewarded the most successful warriors. The heads of sacrifices were often severed and placed on display in a public place.

ANIMAL SACRIFICE

Sacrificial ceremonies did not just involve human beings – dogs, jaguars, and other animals were bred specifically for sacrifice, and many other offerings were also made, including jewels, feathers, and flowers. The scale of Aztec human sacrifice is difficult to judge due to the paucity of archaeological evidence. The Aztecs themselves claimed that 80,400 people were sacrificed when the great pyramid at Tenochtitlan was reconsecrated in 1487, but they may have exaggerated the scale of their rituals in order to impress and intimidate their enemies. Modern experts' estimates for the total number of sacrifices carried out by the Aztecs range from 300 victims per year to a staggering 250,000 per year.

MONTEZUMA II

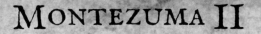

Montezuma II was the ruler of the Aztecs at the time of the Spanish invasion led by Cortes, and had proven himself to be a brave warrior in previous wars. However, the Aztecs were conquered by a relatively small Spanish force, which gave rise to the myth that Montezuma actually thought that Cortes was the returning god Quetzalcoatl, and this is why the Aztecs were so easily defeated. The story suggests that the Aztecs were rendered passive by their own mythology, believing the destruction of their empire was divine destiny. It is said that many portents of disaster had preceded Cortes's arrival, and that Cortes himself bore an uncanny resemblance to the images of Quetzalcoatl that the Aztecs worshipped.

In truth, the Spanish victory was due to a variety of reasons unrelated to the Aztec belief system (the Spanish were better armed, they brought diseases such as smallpox, and the Aztecs were not used to fighting wars in the European style, for example).

FALL OF AN EMPIRE

The legend that the Aztecs believed their conquerors were returning gods seems to have first appeared some 50 years after the conquest, in the Florentine Codex which described the events from a Spanish perspective. The myth also suited the descendents of the Aztec empire, as it helped to explain how they could be

ABOVE: The Encounter between Hernan Cortes (1485-1547) and Montezuma II (1466-1520) from *Le Costume Ancien ou Moderne* by Jules Ferrario, 1820.

defeated despite their enemy's vastly inferior numbers. There is no real evidence, however, that the fall of the Aztec empire was due in any way to their belief in the return of Quetzalcoatl. A similar legend is told about the fall of the Inca empire (see page 138), with the last Inca emperor Atahuallpa mistaking the Spanish General Pizarro for the Inca creator god Viracocha. Again, there is no concrete evidence to support this notion, and it appears to have been invented to explain the conquest long after the event.

Montezuma was said to have been stoned to death by his own people after appearing on the balcony of his palace and ordering his countrymen to retreat rather than fight the Spanish. Another legend tells that Cortes killed Montezuma by pouring molten gold down his throat, thus simultaneously drowning, burning and suffocating him. No definitive account of his death exists, but most scholars believe he was probably killed by the Spanish once they realized that he was unable to pacify the indigenous population.

Montezuma was succeeded by his brother Cuitlahuac, whose rule was cut short when he succumbed to smallpox. His 18-year-old nephew Cuauhtemoc then took the throne but proved unable to resist the Spanish advance and was captured by Cortes whilst trying to escape the besieged city of Tenochtitlan. Cortes allegedly tortured Cuitlahuac by placing his feet in a fire, in an (unsuccessful) attempt to persuade Cuitlahuac to reveal the location of the Aztec's gold.

INCA MYTHOLOGY

The extensive records of the mighty Inca empire were burned by the conquering Spanish on the orders of their Christian priests, so we have to rely on the accounts of the invaders themselves, and the iconography painted on a few historical artefacts in order to piece together the myths they told. Thankfully a few legends have been passed down amongst the native cultures that survived the invasion, and the painstaking work of modern archaeologists has also begun to shed some light on the mysteries of the Inca gods.

INCA CREATION AND FOUNDATION MYTHS

The creator god Viracocha made the world, according to most Inca accounts of creation, after emerging from the bottom of Lake Titicaca. Along with the world itself, he also created the sky, moon and stars, and then breathed life into stones in order to create the first men. However, the first race that he created were ignorant giants, so he destroyed them all by sending a great flood (another example of a motif that recurs again and again in ancient mythologies).

The second version of the human race were created from pebbles, which Viracocha scattered across the world. He taught men how best to live by wandering amongst them disguised as a lowly beggar. He is said to have disappeared from the earth by walking across the Pacific Ocean (his name translates as 'sea foam' or 'sea fat'). There are many clear parallels between accounts of the life of Viracocha and Manco Capac (see page 136), who was sometimes described as Viracocha's son. The myth of Viracocha may have derived from the tale of Bochica, the creator god of the Chibcha (who occupied what is now Colombia). Bochica also made men and taught them how to live, before destroying them with a flood when they turned away from his teachings. After the Chibcha prayed for forgiveness, Bochica is said to have returned on a rainbow and created the Tequendama Falls to allow the flood water to drain away.

THE FIRST EMPEROR

The single most important figure in the myths of how the Inca Empire itself evolved is Manco Capac, the son of the sun god Inti, and first Sapa Inca (or emperor) of the kingdom of Cusco. He is thought to have ruled the Inca around 1200 CE. There are several versions of the story of how he founded Cusco, the most popular of which telling that he emerged from a cave at Pacaritambo carrying a golden staff, having been instructed to come to earth by his father, the sun. In other versions of the story Manco Capac's father is mentioned as being

Viracocha (the creator god) and he emerges from the depths of Lake Titicaca. In some tales he has brothers, whom he kills in order to seize total power – though in one version he has a single brother who is turned to ice after angering the native tribes the brothers encountered.

The Inca Empire expanded quickly by conquering neighbouring tribes, and many of the deities that these tribes believed in were assimilated into the Inca pantheon of gods. There are thus a bewildering number of deities, some of whom seem to overlap with or contradict one another. One common thread running through Inca beliefs is the concept of three separate worlds – Hana Pacha (the world of the gods), Kay Pacha (the world of man) and Uku Pacha (the underworld, or world of the dead). These three worlds are symbolized by the Chakana, or Inca Cross, and are analogous to the 'tree of life' or 'world tree' found in several other cultures.

ABOVE: Manco Capac founder of the Inca dynasty holding Inti the Sun god in his left hand. 18th century painting called *Genealogia*.

INTI AND INTI RAYMI

Inti, the sun god, was the second most important god after the creator god Viracocha. He was represented by the Inca as a golden disc with a human face, and the Inca had a special role of High Priest of the Sun (or Willaq Umu) who was second in rank only to the Sapa Inca in their social hierarchy. The Sapa Inca claimed direct ancestry from Inti, and was considered Inti's living representative on earth.

Inti and his wife, the moon goddess Mama Quilla, were considered largely benevolent deities, as they gave life and fertility to mankind. Farmers relied on the sun to provide them with good harvests, and so they were especially loyal to Inti.

FESTIVAL OF THE SUN

The ceremony of Inti Raymi (Festival of the Sun) still occurs each year at the winter solstice (around June 24 in the Incan Empire) and today attracts thousands of tourists to Cuzco to witness the spectacle. The modern ceremony, however, only dates from 1944 and is a somewhat theatrical interpretation of the original Inca ceremony. In the time of the Inca, many sacrifices would take place in order to ensure the resurrection of the sun. The Inca would fast for several days before the festival, and abstain from any sexual behaviour. The festival itself would last for nine days, and would be accompanied by feasting, drinking, and dancing.

The world famous Inca ruins at Machu Picchu include an Intihuatana stone which was a common feature of major Inca settlements. The pillar-like stone acted as a 'hitching post of the sun', holding the sun in place on its path across the sky. At midday on the equinoxes the sun stands directly above the Intihuatana stone, meaning it casts almost no shadow.

CATEQUIL

The Inca god of thunder and lightning, Catequil, was said to create thunder by banging on the clouds with his mighty clubs. The Inca often carried an idol of Catequil into battle. Catequil was also considered to be an oracle who foretold the future, and a powerful cult grew up around him centred around the foothills of the Cerro Ichal mountain in the north-west of Peru. The Augustinian priests who later attempted to stamp out the belief in Catequil actually preserved the legends associated with him by meticulously recording the beliefs of the Inca in their journals.

From these records we know that the religious settlement at Cerro Ichal was burned to the ground by Atahualpa (the last Sapa Inca) after the oracle Catequil ruled against Atahualpa in his ongoing dispute with his half-brother Huascar over who should rule the Inca. Catequil answered questions put to him through the mouths of the priests of Cerro Ichal, and when Atahualpa was told that Catequil had predicted his defeat, and had also criticized him for killing so many people, he oversaw the systematic destruction of Catequil's shrine in a process that took some three months. Other accounts suggest that Catequil predicted the victory of the invading Christian army, but all seem to agree that Atahualpa responded by destroying the settlement at Cerro Ichal, and by beheading the high priest that Catequil had spoken through. In one account the priest's bones were also ground to powder and then scattered.

Modern excavations of the ruins of the site at Cerro Ichal have revealed that the Inca built sophisticated water channels that may have been used to pass water over sacred stones in order to produce a burbling sound. It is possible that the sound of the water passing over the stones gave Catequil a 'voice' that could be understood and translated by the priests.

THE IDOL OF CATEQUIL

There are some suggestions that the priests of Cerro Ichal rescued the idol of Catequil (or at least several broken pieces of it) and transported it to Cahuana (or perhaps Tauca), where they built a new temple for it. Two Augustinian priests were said to have found the temple and destroyed it, throwing the idol into a nearby river. Other accounts claim the priests hid the idol and it remains undiscovered to the present day. What seems clear is that despite Atahualpa's best efforts, the cult of Catequil survived and spread to neighbouring Ecuador. Augustinian priests reported that the indigenous population gathered stones that they believed to be the sons of Catequil, and they destroyed many hundreds of these in a concerted attempt to stamp out the cult.

As well as foretelling the future, it was believed that Catequil could also force other gods to speak, and so his help was sought whenever the Inca wished to know the views of other gods. Catequil could also turn himself into a bolt of lightning and enter a woman who was making love to her husband. This, the Inca believed, is how women gave birth to twins.

HUMAN SACRIFICE IN INCA CULTURE

Though not nearly as bloodthirsty as the Aztecs, the Inca did offer human sacrifices on important occasions, and seemed to favour the sacrifice of children rather than adults in a practice known as Capacocha. Ice mummies found at the top of the Llullaillaco volcano (on the border between Chile and Argentina) suggest that children were fattened up on special diets of llama meat and maize before sacrifice. The Inca appear to have believed that if sacrifices were offered at high altitudes they would be closer to the gods. The sacrificed children may have been drugged with coca leaves before being suffocated, struck on the head or left to die of exposure.

Major events, such as the death of a Sapa Inca, were marked with more wide scale human sacrifices. It is believed that after the death of the ruler Huayna Capac in 1527, some 4,000 individuals were sacrificed, many of them servants, court officials or concubines.

The earlier Moche culture of northern Peru, who flourished from around 100 CE to 800 CE also practised human sacrifice on a wide scale. Ceremonial fights were staged, and the loser was stripped and bound before being taken to the place of sacrifice. Many of the victims were bled to death, with the blood then being offered up to the gods.

ABOVE TOP: Polychrome frieze representing the face of Aipaec a Moche God, Temple of the Moon, northern Peru. ABOVE LEFT: Human mummy dating back to pre Incan times. ABOVE RIGHT: Face of an Incan mummy sacrificed 500 years ago.

NAZCA MYTHOLOGY

The Nazca flourished from around 1,100 BCE to 750 CE and whilst much of their culture is shrouded in mystery, archaeological investigations from Cahuachi (in modern day Peru) have revealed tantalizing glimpses into their belief systems. Cahuachi appears to have been a largely ceremonial site and was probably a place of pilgrimage, with only a very small permanent population. From Cahuachi it would have been possible to view the famous Nazca lines marked out in the Nazca desert. These lines, or geoglyphs, stretch for some 800 miles (1,300 kilometres) and depict stylized images of a wide variety of birds and animals, including humming birds, spiders, monkeys, and sharks or whales. Several of the creatures depicted have never lived in the area inhabited by the Nazca.

PAMPA COLORADAN

The lines were created by selectively removing the red pebbles of the desert (Pampa Coloradan or Red Plains) to reveal the white earth beneath. From the ground the shapes are not evident – they can only be seen from above. This has led some to speculate that they were designed to be viewed by the gods, rather than by humans. Some have even suggested that the lines are evidence of visitation by aliens from other planets.

Alien influence is of course unlikely, and most experts agree that since the Nazca believed their gods resided in the sky they wanted the Nazca lines to be visible to them, but since no written records of Nazca mythology have ever been found the exact meaning of the geoglyphs remains a mystery. Symbols painted on Nazca pottery suggest that their gods were linked to agriculture and fertility, and nature spirits who have a combination of animal and human features are common. Nazca pottery and textiles are of an astonishingly high standard, and one theory posits that the same grid system used by modern day artists to copy sketches into full-size works of art may also have been used by Nazca's artists to create the giant geoglyphs. However the lines were made, it has been estimated that many hundreds of individuals must have laboured for decades in order to complete them. The dry and calm desert environment has meant that erosion since their creation has been minimal, though recently concerns have been raised about the damage being done to the lines by the thousands of tourists who visit them annually.

HALLUCINOGENIC ART?

It is believed that the Nazca, in common with the contemporary Moche culture of northern Peru (see page 141), used hallucinogenic drugs – possibly extracted from local cactus trees – to induce visions. Some of the images found on Nazca artefacts, and within the Nazca lines themselves, may represent the visions of their shamans.

The Nazca also appear to have been head hunters who took trophy heads from the enemies they defeated in war. Many skulls have been found with holes drilled in them to allow them to be threaded with rope and used as display pieces.

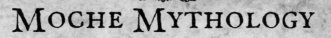

MOCHE MYTHOLOGY

Little is known of the Moche people who inhabited the northern part of Peru at around the same time as the Nazca, but we do know from archaeological excavations that they were involved in ritual human sacrifice and possibly cannibalism. The most famous figure associated with Moche culture is nicknamed The Decapitator because it features a figure holding a knife in one hand and a severed head in the other. Most commonly the figure resembles a spider, but examples have also been found of Decapitators that resemble winged creatures or sea monsters. It is thought that the three types of Decapitator may relate to gods or goddesses of the land, air, and sea.

Human remains found at Moche sites show evidence that their flesh and organs had been removed before burial. As the overwhelming majority of the bodies are those of young males, it has been posited that they represent prisoners of war who may have been butchered and sacrificed for ceremonial purposes.

ABOVE: Photograph of gold silver and gilded copper metalwork treasure jewellery buried in the Moche Mochica royal tomb of Old Lord Sipan in the Lambayeque Valley of Northern Peru. The heads are beads for necklaces worn by the buried warrior priest.

PART 4
ASIA & OCEANIA

In marked contrast with many of the ancient cultures we have looked at, those of India, China, and Japan have a long and well-established practice of writing down their myths and legends, and thus much of their mythology has survived to the present day more or less intact. Gods and goddesses of great antiquity have been faithfully documented and passed down through the generations. With regards to the myths of Oceania we are less fortunate, though an unbroken tradition of storytelling in Aboriginal culture does provide us with the essence of a unique and magical world view.

INDIA

Hindu mythology evolved from the earlier Vedic myths, many of which are outlined in the Rigveda, a collection of Sanskrit hymns dating from around 1000 BCE. The Rigveda is one of the four Vedas (sacred texts) of Hinduism. The Vedic pantheon of gods was vast, and the Hindu belief system appears to have consolidated and streamlined many of the deities to provide a set of stories that is much easier to follow.

INDRA

In the Rigveda there are more stories about Indra than any other god, illustrating his importance in Vedic (and later Hindu) culture. Indra evolved from a god of the Aryan invaders of north India, who in turn may have been based on a real-life mortal who was deified by his loyal followers. A bawdy and often badly behaved god with a giant appetite for food and sex, he provides rich source material for some of the most engaging stories in Indian mythology.

THE GOD OF RAIN AND THUNDER

Known as the God Of Rain And Thunder, Indra is credited with bringing rainfall to India and banishing Ahi (or Vritra), the serpent God Of Drought. Ahi had drunk all of the world's water and coiled himself on top of a mountain. In response, Indra attacks him with thunderbolts which cut Ahi open and release the waters back into the world. He is often depicted riding in a golden chariot, or upon the back of a war elephant, as it is said this is how he first entered the world, preceded by a loud rumble of thunder. In some accounts he was born fully grown from his mother's side.

The great sage Gautama placed a curse on Indra after Indra seduced Gautama's wife, and as a result of the curse a thousand phalluses sprouted all over Indra's body. These later became a thousand eyes and Indra was instead cursed to lose his testicles, which he replaced with those of a ram.

Indra's importance waned as time went on and modern Hindus see him as a relatively minor deity. A rainbow is referred to as 'Indra's bow' in Hindu mythology.

ABOVE: 19th century illustration of Indra the Hindu god of light.

THE TRIMURTI

In Hindu belief, universal order is maintained through a trinity of gods – Vishnu (god of preservation), Shiva (god of destruction) and Brahma (the creator god who mediates between Vishnu and Shiva). Collectively the three gods are known as the Trimurti, and between them they are responsible for all creation and destruction that occurs in the world. Within Hinduism, some followers reject the concept that all three gods are equal, with some placing more importance on one of the three (usually either Vishnu or Shiva) and suggesting the other two are subordinate, or simply different names for the same god.

Brahma seems to have evolved from the Vedic creator god, and in some myths he is said to have created the world by depositing a seed in water, which later grew into a golden egg. Other stories suggest he was born in a lotus flower which grew in the navel of Vishnu, or that he was born in water. Though one of the three Trimurti, Brahma is not nearly as widely worshipped by Hindus as Vishnu and Shiva. This lack of worship is said by some to relate to a curse placed on Brahma by either Shiva or a sage (there are several different versions of the story). He is believed to have a life-cycle of many millions of years, and when he reaches the end of this cycle there will be a gap of 100 of his years before the cycle begins again with a new Brahma creating a new world.

VISHNU AND SHIVA

Vishnu is considered by many Hindus to be the supreme god, and from his light the universe itself came into existence. When descending from heaven, where he lived amidst the lotus flowers with his wife Lakshimi, he would take on earthly forms, known as avatars. These included animal forms such as a fish, tortoise, and boar, as well as human forms. In human form he walked amongst men as Rama, Krishna, and Buddha. It is believed that Vishnu has ten avatars, and that he has thus far used nine. He will use his last avatar to visit the earth again at the end of time, when Kali Yuga, the last of the four world cycles, is complete.

In some Hindu traditions, Shiva reigns as the supreme god, but he is a deity of major importance to all Hindu followers. He shares many characteristics with the earlier Vedic gods Rudra (who was associated with howling or roaring storms) and Indra (both Shiva and Indra have a taste for soma, a divine intoxicating drink). He is commonly depicted with a third eye, and it is said he used this as a weapon to burn kama – desire – to ashes. Shiva's character is somewhat contradictory, as he creates through destruction, and can unify through shattering. At the end of each cycle of the universe it is Shiva who destroys the world, for example, in order for a new one to begin. His frenzied dance is said to precede this act, and many representations of Shiva depict him dancing (often with four arms).

RIGHT: The Trimurti – Brahma, Vishnu and Shiva.

THE MAHABHARATA

One of two epic Hindu poems, *The Mahabharata's* 1.8 million words are believed to have been dictated by the immortal sage Vyasa, who is himself a major character in the work, and who some believe was an incarnation of Vishnu. Ganesha, the jovial elephant-headed god of literature, is said to have written down Vyasa's words. The text seeks to describe four goals of life that Hindus should pursue, as well as discussing many historical events from India's past. It is a vast, sprawling, and often chaotic work, but within its pages are stories that are deeply cherished by all Hindus.

The core of the tale is a battle between two sets of cousins, the Kaurava and the five brothers of the Pandava, for the right to rule the kingdom of Hastinapura (in the modern day Indian state of Uttar Pradesh). Conflicts of loyalty, kinship, and friendship ensue amongst the main characters. After the great 18 day battle of Kurukshetra, the Pandava branch of the family is victorious. Having seen so much carnage, however, the Pandavas renounce everything and, dressed only in rags, climb the Himalayas to try and reach heaven, with a stray dog in tow. One by one they fall, until only Yudhisthira, who had tried to prevent the bloodshed between the families, remains. The stray dog then reveals himself to be the god Yama, and he takes Yudhisthira to the underworld to visit his wife. When the visit is over, Yama takes Yudhisthira to heaven and assures him that his family will join him once they have served their penance in the underworld.

THE FOURTH AGE

Gandhari, the mother of the Kaurava, curses Krishna (Vishnu's eighth avatar) to witness the same cataclysmic destruction of his family as she has just witnessed, for although he had the divine power to stop the slaughter he did nothing. *The Mahabharata* ends with the death of Krishna, and the beginning of the fourth and final age of mankind.

One of the most famous scenes in *The Mahabharata*, the *Bhagavad Gita*, or *Song of the Blessed Lord*, involves Krishna explaining to Arjuna (one of the Pandavas) his duties as a warrior. Arjuna is facing many of his cousins and dear friends across the battlefield before the battle of Kurukshetra, and is thrown into moral confusion. Krishna uses many examples and analogies to expand upon the central teachings of Hindu philosophy, and the *Bhagavad Gita* is considered by many to be a concise introduction to the main tenets of Hindu theology. Krishna explains to Arjuna that souls are eternal, whilst all the physical bodies that might be lost on the battlefield are merely temporary. Arjuna is allowed to briefly see his universal form rather than his bodily form, and is persuaded that in order for truth to triumph over disorder he must take action.

DAMAYANTI AND NALA

This love story is one of the best loved in *The Mahabharata*, and tells of how the beautiful princess Damayanti falls in love with King Nala after hearing about his virtues from a golden swan. Damayanti is so beautiful, however, that even the gods want to marry her, and they disguise themselves as Nala and ask her to choose between them. Damayanti selects the real Nala to be her husband, recognizing him because, as a mere mortal rather than a god, he is not perfect.

ABOVE: *Damayanti Choosing a Husband* by Warwick Goble (1862–1943).

NALA – THE UGLY DWARF

The demon Kali also wishes to marry Damayanti and, jealous of Nala, he curses Nala with an addiction to gambling. Nala loses everything by playing dice with his brother Pushkara, and he and Damayanti are forced to live in abject poverty in a forest. Nala then abandons Damayanti to try and protect her from his bad luck. He is turned into an ugly dwarf after being bitten by the snake king, Karkotaka, after saving Karkotaka's life. Karkotaka explains to the confused Nala that the real venom of the bite will only take effect when the time is right.

Damayanti and Nala are reunited when Damayanti decides to remarry and has to choose a new husband. Although Nala is now an ugly dwarf, she recognizes him because of a dish he cooks for her. The venom of Karkotaka's bite takes effect and Nala vomits the demon Kali, which transforms Nala back into his former shape. Now educated in the skills of playing dice, he wins back his kingdom and he and Damayanti live happily ever after.

ABOVE: Relief of Rama the hero of the Ramayana, Loro Jongrang, Prambanan, UNESCO World Heritage Site, Java, Indonesia.

THE RAMAYANA

Attributed to the great Hindu sage Valmiki, *The Ramayana* – which translates as Rama's Journey – is the other great epic Hindu poem and tells the story of Rama, the seventh incarnation of Vishnu, and his quest to rescue his wife Sita from the demon Ravana. Along with *The Mahabharata* it is one of the most important myths in the Hindu canon, and its 24,000 verses are believed to be set in a period between the 8th and 4th centuries BCE (though the earliest surviving texts date from around the 11th century CE).

Rama, the hero of the story, is the eldest son of Dasharatha, the king of Ayodhya. He is the seventh incarnation of Vishnu, who has opted to become a mortal in order to defeat the fearsome Ravana, a demon who has been bestowed with the gift of invincibility from the power of any god. Rama's brother Lakshmana is his constant companion throughout the story.

A DEMON SISTER

Rama marries Sita, the beautiful daughter of King Janaka, after proving himself the only man capable of wielding Janaka's immensely heavy bow (previously given to Janaka by Shiva). Their marital home is visited by Surpanakha, the demon sister of Ravana, and she attempts to seduce the brothers Rama and Lakshmana. The virtuous brothers refuse her advances, and Lakshmana cuts off her nose and ears. Surpanakha's brother Khara brings a demon army to avenge her, but Rama defeats the entire 14,000-strong army and slays Khara.

Word of this reaches Ravana, who then plots to kidnap Sita, which he manages to do by distracting the two brothers and then tricking Sita into letting him into her house. He takes Sita to Lanka, his island fortress (known in the modern-day as Sri Lanka). Discovering that Sita is missing, Rama and Lakshmana set out upon an epic quest to find her and bring her home.

MONKEY BRIDGE

The brothers arrive at the monkey citadel of Kishkindha, where Rama helps the monkey hero Hauman regain his kingdom, and in return receives Hauman's help to find Sita. Hauman locates Sita in Lanka and offers to rescue her, but she refuses to be touched by any male other than her husband. Rama journeys to the south coast of India, and Hauman's monkeys build a bridge for him to cross to Lanka. The monkeys and demons engage in a fierce battle, which climaxes with Rama and Ravana joining in single combat. An epic struggle sees the two inflict grievous injuries upon each other, with Rama severing Ravana's head, only to see a new one grow back in its place. Finally, Rama invokes the power of Brahma's deadliest weapon, the Brahmastra, and fires an arrow which kills Ravana.

Sita is required to perform a 'test of fire' in order to prove that she was faithful to Rama whilst imprisoned by Ravana. She passes the test and the two return triumphantly to their home. Many years pass peacefully, but rumours that Sita was not faithful to Rama persist, and he banishes her to the forest for a period of 15 years. Upon her return, Rama accepts that he is the father of her children, and Sita, content that her children have been accepted by their father, asks mother earth to swallow her. Shortly afterwards Rama is told that the mission of his incarnation is complete, and he returns to the heavens.

KAMA

ama (sometimes known as Kamadeva) is the Hindu deity of love, and the famous compendium of sexual writings, the *Kama Sutra*, takes its name from Kama, meaning love. He is generally depicted as a handsome young man with a bow made of sugarcane strung with honeybees, firing arrows decorated with five types of fragrant flowers. Kama is married to Rita, the goddess of desire, and often flies on the back of a parrot (or peacock). He is associated with spring, and gentle breezes.

LOSS OF LOVE

The most famous story involving Kama begins with the other gods deciding that it is time for Shiva to remarry after the death of his first wife Sati. They decree that Sati should be reincarnated and she is sent to woo Shiva as Parvati. However, Shiva has dedicated himself to spiritual learning and, living a monastic life in the Himalayas, refuses to be seduced by Parvati. The gods engage the services of Kama to try and arouse some passion in Shiva, and he journeys to the Himalayas to fire one of his arrows of desire into Shiva's heart. Once the arrow strikes Shiva he notices Kama hiding in the bushes nearby and uses his third eye to burn Kama to a pile of ash. Though Shiva does indeed fall in love once again with Parvati, nobody else falls in love with Kama, now dead.

Kama's wife Rita beseeches Parvati to persuade her new husband Shiva to allow Kama to live again. Shiva reluctantly agrees to the request and Kama is reborn as Pradyumna, the son of Krishna and Rukmani, and eventually he and Rita marry again.

ABOVE: The Hindu god Shiva blasting Kama, god of love, with fire from his third eye. Kalighat painting, circa 1885.

THE KAMA SUTRA

The translation of the *Karma Sutra* into English in 1883 reawakened interest in the book both in the West and in India, where its contents had been heavily suppressed for many years. Since then it has become synonymous with ancient wisdom on the subject of sexual intercourse, an almost legendary manual of sex.

The original *Kama Sutra* discusses much more than the physical act of lovemaking. Within its pages are guides to behaviour between married couples, with subjects as diverse as selection of partner and decoration of the home being highlighted as just as important as the positions of lovemaking described in the text. The *Kama Sutra* also has nothing to do with tantric sex, which is a much later belief system in which sex is seen as a path to spiritual enlightenment. Nor is the original text illustrated – illustrations first appeared in editions from the 15th century.

SIXTY-FOUR SEXUAL POSITIONS

Sex is organized into eight distinct topics – embracing, kissing, scratching, biting, sexual positions, moaning, women playing the man's part, and oral sex. Each of these has eight manifestations, giving a total of 64 ways to make love. These are often erroneously described as 64 sexual positions.

Little is known about Vatsyayana, the author of the *Kama Sutra*, but he is believed to have lived in the 3rd century. Vatsyayana built his work from seven earlier Hindu treatises on love, all since lost.

ABOVE: A suitor aiming at his beloved a flower-tipped arrow like that used by Kama, god of love. Indian manuscript illumination, Bilaspur, circa 1750.

CHINA

The earliest Chinese myths are believed to date from the 12th century BCE, having been handed down orally until the adoption of writing and the creation of the first books containing the traditional stories around the 2nd century BCE Many of the myths that were written down were relatively short, and were retold in a relatively prosaic style very different from that of the lyrical poets of ancient Greece. Other myths were turned into plays or novels, and passed down through performances. Because of the piecemeal manner in which Chinese myths were collected into anthologies, the perception outside of China has often been that it is a culture with only a sparse repertoire of myths. The truth is very different: like the country itself, China's treasury of myths is vast, diverse, and exotic.

CHINESE CREATION MYTHS

The most widely told Chinese creation myth is that of Pangu, who emerges from Hundun, the 'world egg' of chaos and nothingness, and separates the two halves of the egg into heaven and earth. All that is light and bright in Hundun becomes the heavens, and all that is dark and heavy becomes earth. Heaven, earth, and Pangu all grow by 3m (10 feet) a day until, with Pangu standing between the two, heaven and earth are separated by a huge distance. In some versions of the story, Pangu is assisted in his task of separating the heavens and the earth by various animal companions including a turtle, a phoenix, and a dragon. Pangu himself is depicted as a hairy giant, with horns sprouting from his head.

HAND CRAFTED HUMANS

After 18,000 years the earth has widened to its current size and the sky is its current distance from the earth. At this point Pangu dies, and the various parts of his body become absorbed into the universe. His eyes become the sun and the moon, his breath becomes the wind and the fleas on his fur become all the animals of the world. The goddess Nuwa then fashions human beings from the mud of a water bed. Some are handcrafted by Nuwa, and these become intelligent nobles, others are simply made from blobs and these become commoners. A different version of the story omits Nuwa and tells that human beings, like the animals, came from the fleas on Pangu's fur.

It is believed the creation story of Pangu is a comparatively late addition to the canon of Chinese myth, and was probably imported from neighbouring cultures, which makes the Chinese unusual in not having a clearly established creation myth of their own.

THE THREE SOVEREIGNS

The emergence of civilization in China is attributed in large part to Fu Xi (or Fushi), husband of Nuwa, and first of the Three Sovereigns who are said to have ruled over China in the prehistoric period. Fu Xi taught humans how to hunt and fish, and how to fashion tools and weapons from iron. He is also said to have invented writing (though other sources claim writing was invented by the official historian of the Yellow Emperor). Many sources state that Fu Xi was the author of the famous divination system the *I Ching* (the *Book of Changes*)

Fu Xi ruled for 115 years and died at the age of 197. His mausoleum at Chen (in modern day Huaiyang county) is now a tourist attraction.

ABOVE: Pangu, the first living being and creator of all things in Chinese mythology, holding Yin-Yang, the symbol of Heaven and Earth.

THE JADE EMPEROR

An alternative creation myth features the deity The Jade Emperor, Yu Huang, although he is credited only with the creation of humankind, rather than the universe. In this version it is The Jade Emperor, rather than Nuwa, who fashions human beings out of clay. As he left his creations to dry in the sun, a sudden storm caused it to rain, leaving some of the figures misshapen. This is the origin of sickness, disease, and deformity in human beings.

The Jade Emperor is considered to be the ruler of heaven, earth and the underworld. It is said that when he was born a light glowed from him which filled the entire kingdom. As his foster-father was the emperor Ching Te, Yu Huang could have ascended to his throne but chose instead to live a life of quiet contemplation, cultivating his Tao in a mountain cave. According to legend, he remained in the cave for a period of several million years. Unbeknownst to The Jade Emperor, a demon was also meditating in another mountain cave for a similar period of time. The demon planned to increase its power in order to conquer the gods of heaven (The Three Pure Ones) and take control of the universe.

INVINCIBLE DEMON

The demon emerges from his cave, confident of his invincibility, and does battle with The Three Pure Ones. The battle appears to be going in favour of the demon, until The Jade Emperor emerges from his mountain cave and, noticing strange lights in heaven, ascends to help The Three Pure Ones in their struggle. With his immense powers of wisdom The Jade Emperor succeeds in defeating the demon, and the other gods pronounce him to be the supreme sovereign.

THE PRINCESS AND THE COWHERD

One of the most popular legends across Asia concerns The Jade Emperor's daughter, Chih'nu (or Zhinu, though in many versions of the tale the heroine is not the daughter of The Jade Emperor and is simply referred to as The Weaver Girl). The tale is closely connected with the Qixi Festival in China, which is sometimes called The Night Of The Sevens as it falls upon the seventh day of the seventh lunar month of the Chinese calendar. The Qixi is a festival of love, during which young women demonstrate their proficiency in domestic arts – melon-carving is especially common – and offer up wishes for loving future husbands.

THE SILVER RIVER

The Weaver Girl weaves colourful clouds in the heavens. Amongst her most fabulous creations is the Milky Way (or Silver River). Every day she descends to earth in order to bathe in a stream. A lowly cowherdsman by the name of Niu Lang comes across The Weaver Girl one day as she bathes (in some versions of the story he has been alerted to her existence by a talking ox). Niu Lang grabs The Weaver Girl's robe and, naked, she is trapped in the stream, unable to return to the heavens. In some versions of the story Niu Lang apologizes to The Weaver Girl and explains to her that the talking ox had told him that if he stole some of her clothes she would have to marry him. In other versions Niu Lang grabs The Weaver Girl and takes her home with him. All versions agree that Niu Lang and The Weaver Girl in time fall in love with one another, and marry. They are happy together and have two children.

A Bridge of Magpies

After a period of several years, The Weaver Girl finds that she misses her father and her homeland in the heavens (though in some versions of the stories the gods demand that she return to the skies). The Weaver Girl ascends to heaven, and the gods move the Silver River far away from earth so that Niu Lang cannot follow her. Seeing how heartbroken this leaves The Weaver Girl,

however, the gods agree that once a year, on the seventh day of the seventh month of the lunar calendar, the two lovers can meet upon a bridge across the Silver River. The bridge is said to be formed by all of the magpies in the world flying up into the heavens on the appointed night. The two lovers are seen in the night sky as the stars of Vega (The Weaver Girl) and Altair (Niu Lang), and the Silver River grows dim at this time of the year, making it appear as though it no longer separates them. Their two children can be seen as two stars shining beside Altair. It is believed that if it rains on the seventh day or the seventh month of the lunar calendar this is The Weaver Girl crying as the magpies have failed to arrive to build a bridge across the Silver River.

ABOVE: Line drawing of the Taoist Trinity also known as the Three Pure Ones – Tao-Chün, Yü-Huang and Lao Tse.

SUN WUKONG – MONKEY

In the West, one of the best known characters from Chinese mythology is Monkey, better known to the Chinese as Sun Wukong or Sun Hou-tzu. A Chinese trickster spirit and king of the monkeys, Monkey plays a prominent role in one of China's greatest novels *Journey to the West* (see page 159).

Born from a fruit stone (or, some say, a stone egg) Monkey had immense strength and could jump and somersault huge distances. He also had an array of special powers, including the ability to transform himself into other shapes (though he often had trouble transforming his tail). Monkey is portrayed a comic character, constantly playing tricks and poking fun at others, and often getting into scrapes that very nearly cost him his life.

AN ARMY OF DEMONS

Monkey is given a job by The Jade Emperor to keep him out of trouble. However the job in question involves watching over the horses of the gods, which is the lowliest job in heaven. Outraged, Monkey rounds up an army of demons and wages war against the heavens. The Jade Emperor appeals to Buddha to help the gods deal with Monkey. Buddha places Monkey on his outstretched palm, and tells him that he can live freely in heaven if he shows he is able to jump further than the end of his hand. Monkey accepts the challenge, aware of his own incredible ability to leap vast distances. He makes a mighty jump, and lands beside five great pillars, which he imagines to be the very edge of heaven. He marks the pillars with urine to prove he has reached them, and then jumps back onto the Buddha's palm to claim his reward. Buddha shows him that the five pillars were in fact Buddha's five fingers, and Monkey has been on Buddha's hand the whole time. Buddha then turns his hand into a mountain, and traps Monkey beneath it.

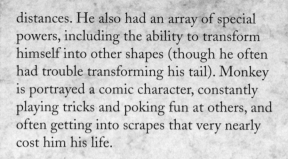

MAGICAL HAIRS

Monkey lies imprisoned beneath the mountain for a period of 500 years. He is finally released after offering to help the young monk Xuan Zang on his quest to retrieve Buddhist scriptures from India. He is told he will be given his freedom if the mission is successful. In order to ensure that Monkey behaves himself during the journey, a magical golden band is placed upon his head which will tighten and cause him great pain if Xuan Zang recites a special chant. Monkey is also given three magical hairs which he is told will help him in his hours of greatest need.

JOURNEY TO THE WEST

Monkey's journey to India with Xuan Zang is described in the epic Chinese tale *Journey to the West*. Published anonymously in the 1590s but usually ascribed to the scholar Wu Cheng'en, *Journey to the West* is one of the most famous novels ever to emerge from China. The story is heavily influenced by China's ancient mythological characters and draws on many traditional tales that were set down generations earlier.

The young Buddhist monk Xuan Zang (who takes the name Tripitaka meaning 'three baskets') sets out on a quest to retrieve Buddhist scriptures from India, with three companions in tow. These companions are Monkey, the pig spirit Zhu Ba Jie and Sha Wu Jing, a former general in heaven who after being exiled to the mortal world became a monster who terrorized the Flowing Sands River. All three companions have been told to serve Xuan Zang in order to atone for earlier sins.

COMPANIONS ON A QUEST

Monkey frequently rescues Xuan Zang from precarious situations and generally assists him to complete his quest successfully. However, the four companions argue constantly on their journey, and Monkey is often at the heart of these disagreements. His great strength is frequently useful, but his propensity for violence does not sit easily with Xuan Zang and the others.

After overcoming countless obstacles and fighting off all manner of demons, Xuan Zang and the others arrive at their destination and receive the holy scriptures in exchange for Xuan Zang's golden begging bowl. Once they have returned the scriptures to China, Xuan Zang and his companions obtain Buddhahood and ascend to heaven.

ABOVE: Illustration from *Journey to the West*, depicting the master being rowed away by a demon in disguise.

THE CHINESE DRAGON

erhaps the most important of all Chinese mythological creatures, and famous throughout the world, the Chinese dragon represents power, strength and good luck – in marked contrast to the sinister dragons prevalent in Western mythology. The Chinese dragon is male, yang, and compliments the female, ying, the mythical bird Fenghuang, which is a phoenix-like creature that reigns over all other birds. The dragon was traditionally the symbol of the Emperor of China, and is

ABOVE LEFT: Dragon design on porcelain vase in workshop in Pingyao, Shanxi, China.

ABOVE RIGHT: Dragon on the roof of Chinese temple.

usually represented as a long, scale-covered creature with no wings, or very small front wings. Although dragons were believed to be able to fly, this gift was considered mystical rather than being related to its anatomical features. Written records of dragons vary in their descriptions of the creatures, with some claiming dragons have a horse's or camel's head, others stating they have horns of a stag or deer, and some mentioning the eyes of a rabbit and the ears of a cow.

SUPERNATURAL POWERS

The list of supernatural powers associated with dragons is almost unlimited. They are said to be able to turn themselves into silkworms, become invisible, turn themselves into water or fire, become as large as the universe, and glow in the dark. The most widespread belief relates dragons to water, as they are seen as rulers of rivers, waterfalls, and seas. In this context there are four main dragon kings, ruling over oceans in the North, East, South, and West of China.

ABOVE: Members of the Chinese community perform a traditional dragon dance in the street of China Town in Manila on February 13, 2010.

YU THE GREAT

Yu was said to have been born from the corpse of his father, Gun, who was executed on the orders of King Shun after failing in his task of preventing the constant floods which beset ancient China. Yu is given the same task and instead of building dykes as his father had done, he dredges new river channels to serve as outlets when the main rivers flood. Yu creates the new rivers, with the help of a yellow dragon and a black turtle (though other versions state that he had 20,000 workers at his disposal too).

According to the legend, Yu was given his epic task just three days after marrying his wife. He is away from home for 13 years in total, but in this time he passes his own home on three separate occasions. On the first occasion he hears his wife in labour. On the second occasion he witnesses his son taking his first steps. On the third occasion he is greeted by his son, now grown into an adolescent. Each time Yu reaches his own home he refuses to enter and spend time with his family, stating that the floods are making others homeless and he will have no rest until all of China is secure.

King Shun was so impressed with Yu's work that he passed the throne on to him rather than to his own son. The throne was then passed on to Yu's son, Qi, creating China's first hereditary dynasty (the Xia Dynasty).

CHINESE ZODIAC STORY

The twelve signs of the Chinese zodiac are the rat, ox, tiger, rabbit, dragon, snake, horse, goat, monkey, rooster, dog, and pig. It is said that they won their places in the zodiac after The Jade Emperor – or in some versions Buddha – organized a race between all the animals on earth.

The rat comes first in the race after hitching a ride on the back of the ox in order to cross a river, then jumping down in front of the ox at the finish line. En route the rat pushes the cat into the river, which is why the two are sworn enemies. The tiger, a strong swimmer, finishes next, followed by the rabbit which reveals it hopped across stepping stones to cross the river quickly. The dragon flies across but, having had to stop in order to make the clouds rain for humankind, only finishes fifth. The galloping horse is about to finish next, until it notices that the snake has hidden in its hoof. Startled, the horse falls backwards, allowing the snake to finish ahead of it in sixth place. The goat, monkey and rooster arrive next, having helped each other to cross the river. The dog finishes next despite being one of the best swimmers, because it spent too long enjoying a bath in the river. The pig is the last to make it into the zodiac, having had a large meal and a nap before getting to the finish line.

RIGHT: The Chinese Zodiac with the characters and images of the twelve animals representing the twelve zodiacal signs, held in the hands of the demon Mara. In the centre of the circle are the eight buddhist symbols. The image combines Tibetan and Chinese symbolism.

THE SECRET HISTORY OF THE MONGOLS

Believed to have been written sometime in the 13th century by an anonymous author, *The Secret History Of The Mongols* contains the only Mongolian account of the life of Temujin (Genghis Khan), the founding father of the Mongolian Empire. Along with what appears to be a historically accurate biography of Temujin's adult years, however, the text also contains a mythological account of his ancestry and early years.

Temujin's distant ancestors are described as being a blue-grey wolf and a deer. The Secret History describes how their offspring formed the first Mongol clans, in what may be seen as a creation myth relating to the Mongol people.

A DIVINE SIGN

Temujin himself is said to have been born clutching a blood-clot in his hand, which was interpreted as being a divine sign that he was to become a hero. His father, a minor clan-leader, was murdered by the rival Tartars when Temujin was just nine years old. The clan refused to be ruled by Temujin due to his tender years, and Temujin and his family were cast out into the wilderness to fend for themselves. During this period Temujin killed his half-brother after an argument.

In many cultures the name of Genghis Khan became synonymous with savage brutality, and whilst he was undoubtedly a

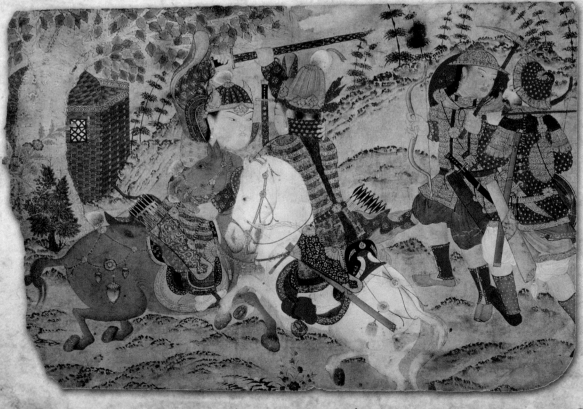

ABOVE: Miniature depicting steppe war of Mongols and Oguz Turkic people, Fatih Album, Topkapi Palace Museum.

ruthless warrior what is largely forgotten is that he was also a man who believed passionately in education, literacy and equality of opportunity. He also inspired such loyalty in his followers that no general ever betrayed him or refused to obey an order.

A DEATH SHROUDED WITH MYSTERY

Temujin's death has also spawned dozens of legends. Most experts appear to agree that he died a peaceful death around his 70th birthday and was buried in secret. Some claim, however, that he died after being struck by lightning, or after a poisoned

arrow struck his knee. One of the more bizarre stories tells of how a mechanical contraption was placed inside the vagina of a Tangut queen that Temujin had captured, so that when Temujin had sex with her the device tore off his genitals.

More legends swirl around his burial. It is said that all those who attended his funeral were later killed to prevent them revealing the location of his grave. Some say that 800 horsemen trampled over the area to obliterate any trace of the grave, and that these horsemen were subsequently executed to ensure they kept their silence.

TIBETAN MYTHS AND LEGENDS

Whilst predominantly a Buddhist culture, the people of Tibet retain echoes of a shamanistic past in their beliefs and ceremonies. There are numerous rites to heal those suffering from sickness, pacify malign spirits and influence the weather, particularly within the Bon tradition which is considered by many to be a distinct religion rather than a branch of Buddhism. Bon beliefs predate Buddhism in Tibet, though they have become heavily influenced by Buddhist thought in recent years.

Followers of the Bon religion, the Bonpo, believe in the fabled land of Tagzig Olmo Lung Ring, which many scholars have equated with the area around Mount Kailash in the north-west of Tibet. Tagzig Olmo Lung Ring is said to be shaped like an eight-petalled lotus flower which is divided into four regions (boundary area, outer area, middle area and inner area).

The land is associated with timeless joy and peace, and can only be reached by those who have attained enlightenment by purifying their body and soul. It is believed to be the birth place of the founder of the Bon religion, Tonpa Shenrab.

The sky of Tagzig Olmo Lung Ring is said to resemble a wheel with eight spokes, and the land itself is dominated by Yungdrung Gutsek (or The Mountain Of Nine Swastikas). This is thought to be Mount Kailash itself, and the same mountain is considered holy across Asia, with Buddhists and Hindus believing that walking around the base of the mountain can wash away the sins of a lifetime (though actually climbing the mountain is strictly forbidden). Bonpo walk counter-clockwise around its base rather than clockwise. Viewed from the south face, a swastika can be seen, and both swastikas and the number nine are considered holy by the Bonpo.

JAPAN

The mythology of Japan is rooted in an amalgamation of the Shinto, Buddhist, and Hindu belief systems, combined with references to countless indigenous folk tales. In Japan the ruling Emperors were elevated to the status of divine beings, so historical fact merges with legend in the stories that describe and explain the events that shaped the nation. The great Japanese texts *The Kojiki* and *The Nihon Shoki* provide a vast store of rich and varied myths which have been handed down intact from the 8th century, as fresh today as they were on the day they were written.

JAPANESE CREATION MYTH

In the most prevalent creation myth in Japan, from chaos and nothingness The Plain of High Heaven emerges. Three gods materialize within the heavens and summon into existence the first two divine immortals, a male, Izanagi, and a female, Izanami. The pair are charged with bringing the earth into existence, and to help them are given a spear (or a pole-like weapon called a naginata).

Standing on the Floating Bridge of Heaven, Izanagi plunges the spear into the primordial waters and strikes mud, which then drops from the end of the spear when he withdraws it. The mud turns into an island that sits on top of the waters, and he and Izanami descend onto it and make it their home. They build a great pillar, and a palace, and then decide to mate and produce offspring. Their first attempt to mate involves them walking around the pillar in different directions until they meet one another, at which point Izanami greets Izanagi, and the two of them make love. However, the two children of this union, Hiruko and Awashima, are deformed, and Izanami and Izanagi put them in a boat made of reeds and send them out to sea. The gods tell them that their offspring are imperfect because Izanami greeted Izanagi, when in order to reproduce the male should instead greet the female.

THE EIGHT ISLANDS OF JAPAN

Izanagi and Izanami walk around the pillar in opposite directions again, but this time when they meet it is Izanagi who greets Izanami. They mate, and their eight children become the eight islands of Japan. They then produce a vast pantheon of deities to rule over the land and seas, too numerous to list in full.

Back on earth, Izanami dies whilst giving birth to the deity of fire, Kagutsuchi. Izanagi attempts to revive her, and is partially successful, but Izanami has lost all desire for life. From her dying body, however, numerous new deities spring forth. A goddess is also born from the tears that Izanagi sheds for his wife.

After Izanami is buried on Mount Hiba, Izanagi kills Kagutsuchi in a grief-stricken rage, but this action only creates even more deities who emerge from various parts of Kagutsuchi's body. Izanagi continues to mourn bitterly for his departed wife, until he can bear the pain of separation no longer and resolves to journey to Yomi (the underworld) to find her.

IZANAGI'S JOURNEY TO THE LAND OF YOMI

In common with many of the other cultures highlighted in this collection, Japanese mythology features a story in which a hero visits the land of the dead. The hero in this case is Izanagi, who longs to rescue his dead wife from the underworld.

Izanagi has to journey many thousands of miles to reach the underworld, but he finally arrives at the gates of a castle which he knows at once is the entrance to the realm where the deceased Izanami now resides. With the front of the castle guarded by fearsome demons, he runs around to the back of the castle and looks for his wife. Yomi is a land of darkness, but Izanagi manages to catch sight of Izanami, and calls out to her. Izanami tells her husband that she cannot return to the earthly realm as she has already eaten the food of the underworld. Izanagi begs her to find a way to return to him, and Izanami replies that whilst she cannot leave without the permission of the rulers of the underworld, she will seek that permission on account of Izanagi's incredible devotion at travelling so far to find her. She warns Izanagi, however, that he must not look inside the castle while she is gone. Izanagi agrees and Izanami disappears into the castle.

ROTTING CORPSE

Izanagi waits for many hours but finally his patience is exhausted, and he breaks off the tooth of a comb and lights it in order to see amidst the gloom of Yomi. Fearing harm has come to his wife, he enters the castle and immediately sees Izanami on the floor. The bright light of the comb reveals her to be a rotting corpse, seething with maggots. Horrified, Izanagi flees, and desperately tries to return to the earthly realm, no longer concerned with rescuing his wife.

Izanami swears revenge on him for breaking his word and abandoning her. She sends foul hags to pursue Izanagi and bring him back to Yomi. Izanagi throws his headdress to the ground and it magically becomes a bunch of grapes which the hags trip on, buying him valuable time. He throws his comb to the ground and it becomes bamboo shoots, he urinates against a tree and it becomes a river, and he throws peaches at the hags – all of which delay the hags for long enough to allow Izanagi to reach the exit to Yomi. He rolls a giant boulder over the entrance to the underworld, sealing the dead there forever.

The furious Izanami pledges to kill 1,000 people every single day to take revenge on Izanagi. From that point on, Izanami becomes the goddess of the underworld. Izanagi purifies himself by washing himself in a river, an action which creates yet more deities, including the sun goddess Amaterasu.

AMATERASU AND SUSANOWA

Sun gods, as we have seen, are common in mythology – sun goddesses, however, are much rarer. Amaterasu (literally 'that which illuminates heaven') is one such goddess, and she is also one of the most important deities in Japanese mythology.

Born from Izanagi's eye as he washed his face, Amaterasu was considered so beautiful that she was taken to heaven by the gods where she became the sun. In time, she gave birth to a son, and it is from this son of the sun that all future Japanese Emperors would claim their divine descent.

Amaterasu had two brothers – Tsukuyomi, the moon god, born from Izanagi's other eye, and Susanowa, a storm god, born from Izanagi's nose, who is sometimes called Susanoo. The most famous myth to feature Amaterasu involves a dispute she has with her brother Susanowa.

A DIFFICULT RELATIONSHIP

The relationship between Amaterasu and Susanowa is presented as fractious in many Japanese stories, and the tension between the two comes to a head when they engage in a competition to see who can bring forth the most divine children. Amaterasu creates three women from Susanowa's sword, and Susanowa creates five men from Amaterasu's necklace. The two then argue over who had actually won the contest, since each is partly responsible for each set of creations. Susanowa falls into a terrible rage, and destroys Amaterasu's rice fields before hurling the corpse of a flayed horse (or pony) into the hall of her palace. Amaterasu's hand-maidens are weaving at the time, and the hurled horse smashes their looms, sending splinters into their bodies and killing them.

Amaterasu is so upset by these events that she shuts herself in Amano-Iwato, the heavenly cave, and seals it with a giant boulder. As a result, the whole of the earth is plunged into darkness, and all of the vegetation begins to wither. The other deities realize they have to find a way to lure Amaterasu out of the cave, and so they gather outside the cave and hit upon a plan. A mirror is placed outside the cave entrance, and the goddess of merriment, Uzume, begins to dance whilst beating out a rhythm on an upturned bath tub. Uzume bares her breasts and lifts her skirt, to the great amusement of the other deities. Amaterasu is intrigued by the commotion outside of the cave, and peeks out to see what is taking place. Seeing her own reflection in the mirror, she thinks a beautiful new goddess has arrived, and she emerges from the cave to investigate her. The other deities then seal the entrance to the cave to prevent Amaterasu ever retreating back into it in the future.

Festivals take place around the winter solstice, December 21, in Japan to celebrate Amaterasu emerging from her cave.

THE YAMATO CYCLE AND THE IZUMO CYCLE

The Yamato Cycle of Japanese myths follows Amaterasu, and focuses on the celestial deities, whilst the Izumo Cycle follows her brother Susanowa and the earthly Deities. Each cycle contains numerous stories of the siblings' adventures and the adventures of their offspring. Perhaps the most important member of the family is Susanowa's son-in-law Okuninushi, who as Great Land Master, is the god of nation-building.

The most popular story about Okuninushi involves a journey he makes with his 80 brothers in order to seek the hand of the Princess Yakami. En route, his brothers encounter a skinned hare, lying in agony by the side of the road. They advise the hare to bathe in the saltwater of the sea to help its pain, but this only makes the hare's pain even worse. Okuninushi then finds the hare and advises it to bathe in freshwater and then roll in pollen. This eases the hare's pain and causes its fur to grow back. The hare reveals itself to be a god in disguise, and in gratitude pledges that he will ensure that princess Yakami will be his bride.

Okuninushi's brothers are furious about this and they kill him by heating a boulder and rolling it down a hill towards him. His mother brings him back from the dead, only for his brothers to kill him once again – this time crushing him to death. At this point Okuninushi's mother tells him to seek refuge in the underworld. He does, and falls in love with Susanowa's daughter, whom he later marries.

EMPEROR JIMMU

Japan's legendary first human emperor was descended from Amaterasu, and if the stories of his life are to be believed he was born around 711 BCE Experts are divided over whether the story of Jimmu is based on a real-life historical figure or whether it is pure fiction.

Jimmu and his three brothers head east towards modern-day Osaka, in order to try and unite Japan and become its first rulers. There they fight a series of battles, chiefly against Nagasunehiko (whose name translates as 'long-legged man'). Jimmu's brothers are all killed in the battles, and he himself is at the point of exhaustion in his final battle when suddenly the sky becomes dark and a golden kite flies from the heavens to land upon his bow. Jimmu's enemies are so dazzled by the brightness of the kite that they can no longer fight, and the victorious Jimmu becomes emperor.

Jimmu's victory is celebrated in Japan on National Foundation Day, which also marks New Year's Day in the traditional lunisolar calendar – February 11.

ABOVE: Jimmu Tenno, First Emperor of Japan.

PRINCE OUSU

Usually counted as the 12th Emperor of Japan, Prince Ousu (or Yamato Takeru) is the main protagonist in one of the most widely-known legends of the country.

Ousu slays his brother after a quarrel, and his father, fearful of Ousu's violent nature, sends him to a series of battles in which he hopes Ousu will be killed. Ousu, however, manages to slay his enemies and avoid plots on his life. He famously clothes himself in his aunt's dress, and mixes with a group of concubines in order to gain access to a feast that his father's enemies are enjoying. Once inside he draws his sword and slays them.

Ousu finally dies after being cursed with disease after blaspheming against one of the gods. After his death his soul is said to have turned into a great white bird and flown away.

CHUSHINGURA

Japan's favourite story is based on a series of real events called *The Genroku Ako Incident*, or *The Revenge of the Forty-Seven Ronin*. Censorship in Japan in earlier times forbade the portrayal of current events and so the original story began to be retold in slightly fictionalized form in Kabuki and puppet plays. The tradition of retelling the story continues to this day with films and television dramas, and such fictionalized accounts are called *Chushingura*.

The tale is perhaps the most widely known example of bushido, or the Samurai warrior code of honour. It is set in 1701, and begins with the visit of a court official, Kira, to Edo Castle (in modern-day Tokyo). The ruling shogun (feudal overlord) places Kira in the care of a local daimyo (feudal lord), Asano. In due course, Asano attempts to kill Kira with a short sword, though Kira survives the attack. Exactly what provokes Asano to his actions remains unclear, but it is thought to relate to Kira's ungracious and abusive behaviour towards Asano.

RITUAL SUICIDE

Asano is ordered to commit seppuku (ritual suicide by disembowelment) as a punishment for his crime. After he does so, his lands are confiscated and the 47 samurai who had served him are dismissed, making them ronin (samurai without a master).

The 47 ronin believe they must avenge their master, and so plan to kill Kira. Since he is on his guard after the death of Asano, however, they disperse and for two years take up menial jobs and generally attempt to pretend to have forgotten the incident. The leader of the ronin indulges in a life of debauchery to further throw Kira's spies off the scent. When Kira finally relaxes his guard, however, they reassemble and attack his mansion, slaughtering his own samurai guard and beheading Kira. They then take Kira's severed head to Asano's grave, and, together, commit seppuku.

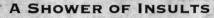

A SHOWER OF INSULTS

Fictionalized *Chushingura* tend to place the events several centuries earlier in Japan's history, and change the names of the main characters in the story. The character of Kira is often exaggerated to make him appear more of a villain, and in some versions of the story he attempts to seduce Asano's wife. When Asano's wife rejects his advances, Kira becomes angry and takes his frustration out on Asano by showering him with insults. Often Asano calls upon his samurai warriors to avenge him as he is in the process of committing seppuku. In some versions he whispers his desire to be avenged to his loyal retainer with his dying breath. One popular variation of the story involves one of the 47 ronin being excused from committing seppuku so that he could live to tell the story to others.

ABOVE: Yodanme Art shows three actors one brandishing a sword. From the series Chushingura juichimai tsuzuki The eleven acts of Chushingura Theater.

INDIGENOUS AUSTRALIA

The stories traditionally told by the Indigenous Peoples of
Australia are commonly known as the Dreamtime Stories
(sometimes known as the Songlines). The myths of each of
the peoples tend to relate to their local landscapes, and are
thus unique to each culture, but a common thread of ancestor
worship and the sacred bond between man and nature link
many of the stories together in a recognizable worldview that
unites all Indigenous Australians.
Some of the stories passed down through the
indigenous cultures are considered sacred and secret.
Other stories are considered to be part of an Indigenous
Australian's education, teaching children the vital skills
they need to progress to adulthood.

ABORIGINAL CREATION MYTH

There is no single unifying Creation Myth of the Indigenous Australian peoples, and different traditions state that different entities were created by different spirits. The most prevalent belief, however, is that the world is eternal, and was created during the time of Dreaming or 'timeless time', when gods and ancestor spirits regularly visited the earth. It is thought that once they finished creating the world, these gods sank back into the earth at various sacred sites, where they remain and their power can be tapped into. However, the earth itself is seen as very much a work in progress, and the Dreaming is thus best thought of as the initial stage of construction of the present world, which continues to change in the present and may yet be radically changed in the future.

THE TWO WISE MEN AND THE SEVEN SISTERS

One story that is very close to a creation myth comes from the Wong-gu-tha people of South Australia.

The creator god, Jindoo (the sun), sends two Spirit Men, Woddee Gooth-tha-rra, from the far end of the Milky Way down to the Earth Yulbrada to create the hills, valleys, lakes, and oceans. Once they have finished their work, Jindoo sends the Seven Sisters (each a star in the Milky Way) to beautify the Earth with flowers, trees, and animals.

As the sisters are busy creating honey-ants, they become thirsty, and the youngest sister is sent to find water. The two Spirit Men, in hiding nearby, follow her, and introduce themselves to her.

SPECIAL POWERS

The youngest sister does not return to the other sisters, and so they go in search of her. They find her with the Spirit Men, and she tells them that she has fallen in love with the men. Jindoo has warned the sisters that if such a thing were to happen, the person who fell in love would be unable to return to the Milky Way. As a result, the other six sisters leave for the Milky Way and the youngest sister remains on the Earth with the Spirit Men.

The special powers of the Spirit Men are taken away from them, and they become the first mortals. These mortals create the rules by which men must live, and their union with the youngest sister creates the first indigenous people. The Wong-gu-tha believe that all of their people are descended from the two Spirit Men and the youngest sister, and thus the stars play a central role in their cultural beliefs.

THE RAINBOW SERPENT

One figure that appears in almost all Aboriginal cultures is the Rainbow Serpent or Rainbow Snake, though its name differs from population to population. The association of a snake-like creature with rainbows may be explained by the fact that bows were not weapons used by the Aborigines. The Rainbow Serpent is closely linked with water, and particularly with rivers and streams, as they meander across the landscape in a snake-like fashion, reflecting the light from the sky. The serpent is itself said to live in water, and to control all the waters in Australia.

A vast and powerful creature, the Rainbow Serpent is said to have created the mountains and valleys by writhing up from beneath the ground. The paths the Rainbow Serpent took across the land later filled with water to become rivers and streams.

A SERPENT WITH TWO SIDES

It is believed that the earthly Rainbow Serpent is the ancestor of a serpent that lives in the Milky Way, visible as a dark line against the bright stars of the night sky. It can be benevolent or malevolent, providing people with healing or striking them down with sores. The stated ability of the Rainbow Serpent to rear up out of deep water and drown people may also have been the inspiration for the legend of the Bunyip.

ABOVE: Rainbow Serpent at the Aboriginal rock art site at Ubirr Rock, Kakadu National Park, Northern Territory, Australia.

THE BUNYIP

Sometimes called the Kianpraty, this large mythical creature is said by the Aborigines to dwell in water holes, rivers, and swamps, and to catch human beings with its fearsome claws before crushing and devouring them. Descriptions of the physical appearance of the Bunyip vary widely, not least because few have encountered them and lived to tell the tale. Some talk of a giant starfish-like creature, while others describe an alligator-like body married to a dog-like or walrus-like face. All seem to agree that it is vast in size and fearsome in temperament.

Early European settlers considered the Bunyip to be a real animal unique to the Australian continent, and several discoveries of the bones of Bunyips were reported throughout the 19th century. One 'Bunyip skull' was displayed at the Australian Museum for two days before being identified as the foetal skull of a calf or foal.

THE SOURCE OF ALL EVIL

Various magical powers are ascribed to the Bunyip, and some Aborigines believe it to be the source of all of the evil in the world. One Aboriginal story states that the Bunyip was originally a man who disobeyed the Rainbow Serpent and was cast out from his tribe, at which point he became an evil spirit. Some female members of the tribe ignored warnings to have nothing to do with the Bunyip and were captured by him and turned into water spirit slaves of the Bunyip. Their beautiful voices were said to lure men to their doom in much the same way as the Sirens of Greek myth.

The word Bunyip is usually translated as 'evil spirit' or 'devil', though in the broader Australian community the word has also come to mean an impostor or fraudulent pretender.

ABOVE: Depiction of the Australian Bunyip lake monster.

THE MOON

In many mythologies, the moon is a powerful deity; however, in one of the most popular Dreamtime myths he is portrayed as a lonely man seeking love from mortals. Different peoples have different versions of the story, but usually the tale explains why the faces of the moon change over time. In these stories, the moon is something of a clown, always making mortals laugh but never managing to woo any mortal females.

Spying two girls paddling across a river, the moon asks them for a lift in their canoe. The girls take pity on the moon and agree to share the canoe with him. Half way across the river, the moon begins to tickle the girls, and as they wriggle and squirm the canoe capsizes. The moon sinks into the river as the girls climb back into the canoe. They watch as his face gradually disappears underneath the water, changing from a bright shining whole to a thin crescent as it sinks into the darkness of the river.

This is why the moon's face is said to change in the night sky. At first he peeps around the corner of the horizon, ashamed of his lust for girls. Then he gradually emerges until his full face is visible, at which point he tries once again to woo mortal women. He always fails, however, and so he gradually fades away again.

THUKERI

Many of the stories that Indigenous Australian communities tell have a clear moral, and such stories are told to children in order to teach them how to behave. The tale of the Thukeri is one such story told by the Ngarrindjeri people of South Australia.

Two men go fishing on Lake Alexandrina in a bark canoe. They catch so many thukeri (bream) that the canoe threatens to sink beneath the weight of the fish. As they paddle the canoe to the shore, a stranger approaches them. The two men hide their fish as they do not wish to share them with anyone. Sure enough, the stranger tells the two men that he has not eaten all day, and he asks them if they could possibly spare a fish for him. The men tell the stranger that they only have enough fish for themselves, as they did not catch very many. As the stranger walks away, he turns and tells the men that because of their greed they will never enjoy thukeri again.

THE GLUTTONY OF MAN

When the two men begin to gut their fish, they find that each fish is full of dozens of small bones, making them almost inedible. They return to their village and explain what has happened. The elders of the village tell the men that the stranger was in fact the spirit Ngurunderi, and that because of the two men's greed all of the Ngarrindjeri will now suffer from his curse.

ULURU

Many legends surround Australia's most famous landmark, though Aboriginal people say that the most sacred of them cannot be told to non-indigenous peoples. Those that are in the public domain relate to the spirits said to dwell at Uluru, and the incidents that have taken place there. Indigenous Australians tend to view Uluru not as a single entity formed in one time and place, but as a landmark formed by several different incidents taking place at different times.

One myth states that Uluru was built by two boys playing in the mud after a rain storm. The two boys piled layer upon layer of mud until Uluru reached its current size. They then slide down its south side on their bellies, digging their fingers into the earth as they slid, creating the great grooves in the rock.

DEAD ANCESTORS SPIRITS

A second myth states that a community had been invited to attend the ceremony of another local community, but could not attend as their own ceremony had already started. Insulted, the second community then sent a fierce dog-like creature (some say a dingo) to attack them, and many of the Uluru community were killed. This provoked a terrible battle between the two tribes, which led to both of the leaders of the tribes being killed. The earth rose up in anguish at the bloodshed, and this is how the great mountain at Uluru was formed. The spirits of the dead are said to still inhabit Uluru.

Another myth states that two serpent beings did battle around Uluru, and as they chased each other around the monument they scarred the rocks, creating the marks that are visible today.

ABOVE: Uluru.

POLYNESIAN CREATION MYTHS

he creator god Tagaloa is believed by Samoans to have made the universe, though there are countless different stories to suggest how he achieved this feat. Some state that he made the world after breaking out of a shell. Another story tells that he sent a vine to earth, and that in time maggots emerged to feed upon the roots of the vine. At this point Tagaloa turned the maggots into animals and humans. Others still say that humans evolved from worms rather than maggots.

ABOVE LEFT: Wood figure of the god Tangoroa in the act of creating the other gods and man. From Rurutu Island, Austral Group, Polynesia. 18th or 19th century. ABOVE RIGHT: Digital illustration of Maui, the great trickster-hero in Maori mythology, hauling fish from ocean floor.

Similar gods (or quite different gods with similar names) exist all across Polynesia. In Tonga, the Tangaloa are an entire family of gods, the first of whom is described as the cousin (or son, or father) of the main creator god Maui, who is said to have dragged the Tongan islands up to the surface from the bottom of the ocean. Maui is also said by the Maori to have 'fished up' the North Island of New Zealand (the South Island is believed to have once been his canoe).

In French Polynesia we find Ta'aroa, another creator god, who is also said to have created the world from the fragments of a shell that he broke out of. Ta'aroa divided the world into seven levels. His children decorated the sky with the sun, moon, and stars.

Wondjina

The Wondjina are water spirits who feature in a flood myth of the indigenous peoples of north and north-western Australia. It is said that the Wondjina helped to create the world, but after a time became upset at how cruel human beings had become. In order to punish the humans, the Wondjina opened their mouths, and torrential rain fell on earth, causing a flood that destroyed much of the world. The Wondjina then recreated the world anew, and their mouths disappeared so that they could not flood the world again.

It is believed that when each Wondjina found a suitable place to die, it painted an image of itself on the rock and then retreated into a water hole, where its spirit remains. Images of Wondjina are still painted (and repainted) on cave walls by Indigenous Australians to ensure that the monsoon rains come each year. Some Wondjina images are over 20,000 years old, and some have been repainted up to 40 times. Only certain specially appointed people are allowed to depict Wondjina on the rocks.

Bullroarer Cults

The Bullroarer is a musical instrument of great antiquity, found all across the ancient world under a variety of different names. In certain Indigenous Australian cultures, the Bullroarer is the foundation of a myth which relates to rites of passage ceremonies for boys about to reach adulthood. The instrument itself is a phallic object threaded with string, which when swung produces a noise.

A Man Thing

It is said that the Bullroarer used to belong to women, until men received the secret of the instrument by trickery. It is now forbidden for women to even hear the sound of the Bullroarer. Young boys are taken to an isolated spot, and the Bullroarer is swung over the heads of the initiants to produce its eerie sound. Newly circumcised boys are also given small Bullroarers to swing in an attempt to promote healing, and to ward off females.

Elsewhere, Bullroarers are used in ceremonies to summon wind and rain, promote fertility and ward off evil spirits. The Polynesian god Sido (see page 186) is said to make plants grow by swinging his penis like a Bullroarer.

DUDEGERA

he name Dudegera translates as 'leg child', and this god from Papua New Guinea got his name from the manner of his birth: he sprang from a cut in his mother's leg (some versions state that he emerged from the spot where his mother's leg brushed against a dolphin's skin). Dudegera was mocked as a child, and in order to seek vengeance on his tormentors he climbed into the sky and transformed himself into the sun. He then threw down spears of sunlight which caused fires to erupt all over the earth, killing many people and destroying much of the earth's vegetation. His mother, hiding beneath a rock, realized she must do something to control her son and so she threw mud up at him (though in some versions it is lime) to try and blind him. The mud turned into the clouds, which protect the earth from Dudegera's fiery spears.

THE TWO TREES

This Micronesian myth has strong parallels with the story of The Garden Of Eden. The spirit guardian Na Kaa lives in a garden of paradise, which he allows human beings to share, as long as they remain under one of two trees. The first tree is for men to sit under, and the second tree is for women. When Na Kaa is called away from the garden, he gathers the two groups together and they become aware of each other's presence in the garden for the first time. Na Kaa tells the two groups to wait for him under their separate trees, but no sooner has he left than the men and women all return to just one tree, where they have sex with one another.

Na Kaa returns and informs the humans that they have chosen to mate under the tree of death, rather than the tree of life. From this point on, human beings become mortal, and only the gods enjoy the tree of immortal life.

MAORI MYTHS AND LEGENDS

Whilst the indigenous people of New Zealand, the Maori, share many of their myths with other Polynesian cultures, they also have several stories that relate to the peoples who lived on the islands of New Zealand before the Polynesian settlers arrived in their canoes.

The creator of humankind is said to be the god of the forests, Tane, who is the son of the sky (Ranginui) and the Earth (Papatuanuku). Tane creates the first woman, Hineahuone, from the sacred soil at Kurawaka. Tane and Hineahuone then have a daughter called Hinetitama, the goddess of dawn and light, and Tane finds her so beautiful that he takes her to be his wife.

Hinetitama later discovers that her husband is also her father and, disgusted, runs off to Po, the underworld. Thereafter she becomes Hine-nui-te-po, the queen of the underworld.

RIGHT: Maori wood art and carving at Whakapapa Tongariro National Park, North Island, New Zealand.

THE CANNIBALS OF VANUATU

The island of Vanuatu in Melanesia has had a reputation for cannibalism for several centuries, and unlike many of the tales described in this book, this account of a people who ate other humans is based largely on fact. The last cannibal killing on Vanuatu occurred as recently as 1969. Warring tribes accounted for most of the cannibalism, but many missionaries who visited the island were also killed and eaten. Traditionally, the people of Vanuatu would bake their victims in a hole in the ground filled with hot rocks.

GOOD AND EVIL

According to a myth told by the people of the Vanuatu Islands, the creator god, Qat (who has close associations with the Polynesian creator god Maui) had twin sons, To Kabinana (the sun) and To Karvuvu (the moon). In one story To Kabinana creates all that is good in the world, and his brother To Karvuvu creates all that is bad. To Karvuvu is not presented as a malicious god in the story, however, he is simply inept. To Kabinana creates the first woman by breathing into a coconut, for example, but when To Karvuvu attempts to follow suit he chooses a coconut that has gone bad, and so the woman he creates is dead. To Kabinana then creates a fish from wood, and when To Karvuvu copies him he accidentally creates the shark.

The story ends with the brothers taking turns to look after the first woman as she grows old. To Kabinana, rather than looking after the old woman, kills her and eats her. This, it is said, marks the origins of cannibalism on Vanuatu.

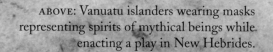
ABOVE: Vanuatu islanders wearing masks representing spirits of mythical beings while enacting a play in New Hebrides.

THE HULI PEOPLE

The Huli are an indigenous people of Papua New Guinea, renowned for their exotic ritual ceremonies, during which they paint their faces in bright colours and wear extraordinarily elaborate wigs created from human hair, flowers, bird feathers and pigments. Many of the wigs are so large they need to be supported with bamboo frames. According to legend, the Huli have in the past partaken in cannibalism, and thus acquired a fearsome reputation amongst early missionaries. The Huli's ancestors were also headhunters, removing the heads of their enemies and bringing them back to their settlements as war-trophies.

POWERFUL SPIRITS

The most powerful spirits in the Huli belief system are the Dama who inhabit both the sky and the Earth, and control everything from the climate to the fertility of the land and all living species. The Dama intervene extensively in human affairs, and can cause sickness and death, though their power can be mitigated or even manipulated by humans if the correct ceremonies are performed.

The less powerful Dinini are the ghosts of the Huli's ancestors. Male Dinini are generally benevolent and seek to protect the living, but female Dinini tend to be malevolent, especially to those outside of their direct family. Whilst Dinini cannot be appeased in the way that Dama can, they can be tricked or thwarted by those who have knowledge of the correct strategies.

Tomia is a force, rather than a spirit being, and it resides in certain material objects such as rocks. The power of Tomia can be harnessed by humans, and used to cause sickness or death in others.

ABOVE: Papua New Guineans of Huli Tribe, Port Moresby Cultural Festival, Port Moresby, Papua New Guinea.

SIDO

In Papua New Guinea, Sido is a fertility god also credited with creating the earth, teaching men to speak, and stocking the seas with fish. One version of the story states that his parents were Siamese twins who became separated by his birth. Portrayed as a trickster god, it is said he could change his skin like a snake, ensuring his immortality, but one night some children spied on him performing this feat and the spell was broken. After he died (some say killed by a magician) his spirit continued to wander the world in search of a wife. He finally married a mortal woman, but when she died Sido transformed into a giant pig. He then split himself open, and the backbone and sides of the pig became the foundations of the underworld, which Sido then proceeded to rule over.

In another form – that of Sosum – it is said that he could make plants grow by swinging his penis like a Bullroarer. The power of fertility erupted from his penis bringing new life not just to plants but to animals and humans beings too. Another version of the story states that he could make fire by rubbing wood across his teeth. Different cultures have various different tales of Sido, and there is some dispute over whether the assortment of different gods who share a similar name are all versions of the same deity or separate, perhaps related, beings.

THE BIRDMAN OF RAPA NUI - EASTER ISLAND

Famous for its enigmatic Moai statues, Rapa Nui is the easternmost of the Polynesian islands and was once home to a thriving indigenous population that largely died out due to a combination of disease and deforestation. One of the most serious blows to the people of Rapa Nui came in 1862, when Peruvian slave traders captured or killed some 1,500 men and women, and later also introduced smallpox to the island. By 1877, some 97 per cent of the population had been killed, captured or otherwise transported from the island.

MYSTICAL STATUES

Whilst all theories regarding the Moai statues remain controversial, the broad consensus amongst experts is that they represented the population's ancestors, who were worshipped in return for their protection. The statues face inland, with their backs to the spirit world in the sea.

It is thought that in time the Ancestor cult made way for the cult of the Birdman (Tangata Manu), who represented Rapa Nui's creator god Makemake in human form on the island. By the time Captain Cook reached the island in the 18th century several of the Moai statues had been toppled, and the competition between islanders to become the Birdman had overshadowed the worship of ancestors in terms of importance. Petroglyphs found on the rocks of Rapa Nui also attest to the key significance of the Birdman.

A DANGEROUS FEAT

The Birdman competition was held annually, and hopefuls for the title appointed a Hopu to physically participate on their behalf. The Hopu would then attempt to retrieve the egg of a Sooty Tern from their nesting sites on the neighbouring islet of Motu Nui, climbing down the cliffs of Rapa Nui and then swimming to the islet before returning back to the cliff top on Rapa Nui with the egg. The patron of the successful Hopu was then crowned as the human representative of Makemake, the god who, it was believed, created humans and tended to their needs on the island. The race to Motu Nui was incredibly dangerous, and many competitors died during the competition – either as a result of falling from the treacherous cliffs, drowning, or being eaten by sharks.

Two rival clans traditionally took part in the Birdman competition – one clan from the east of the island and the other from the west. The winning patron would lead a procession of his followers back to their settlement, and that clan would have the sole right to collect the birds' eggs from Motu Nui for the rest of the season. The Birdman himself would live in seclusion for a year in a special ceremonial house, allowing his fingernails to grow and wearing a headdress of human hair.

ABOVE: Moto Nui Islet, Orongo is a stone village and ceremonial centre at the southwestern tip of Rapa Nui (Easter Island).

INDEX

Page numbers in *italic* denote pictures

PICTURE CREDITS

The publisher would like to thank the following for permission to reproduce photographs:
Cover Images: Mask © Peter Horree / Alamy. Back cover © LOOK Die Bildagentur der Fotografen GmbH / Alamy
Internal Images: Getty Images: 9, 77 © Comstock Images / 10 © Kazuko Kimizuka / 12, 21, 22, 24, 25, 32, 40, 95,
115 © Getty Images / 18 © Herbert James Draper / 16 © After Johann Bernhard Fischer von Erlach / 23, 81 © DEA
/ G. Dagli Orti / 28 © DEA / A. De Gregorio / 31 © Sir Edward Burne-Jones / 35, 184 © Time & Life Pictures/
Getty Images / 39 © General Photographic Agency / 43 © French School / 44 © Italian School / 47 © Daniel
Maclise / 49, 79 © SuperStock / 66 © DEA Picture Library / 84 © Assyrian School / 90 © Martin Gray / 99, 132 ©
Bridgeman Art Library / 104 © PHOTO 24 / 118, 180 R © Dorling Kindersley / 131 © B. Anthony Stewart / 134
© Gallo Gallina / 139 R © Maria Stenzel / 142 © Glowimages / 161 R © AFP/Getty Images / 167 © Demetrio
Carrasco / 179 © Nicole Duplaix. **Alamy:** 20 © ReimarRalph / 51, 57, 159, 171 © Mary Evans Picture Library / 54,
62, 69 © INTERFOTO / 61 © mediacolor's / 63, 145 © The Print Collector / 65 © Charles Stirling / 70, 87, 92,
97 © The Art Archive / 72 © Nikreates / 73 © Robert Harding Picture Library Ltd / 74 © North Wind Picture
Archives / 100, 101 © Black Star / 113 © North Wind Picture Archives / 122 L © Corbis Premium RF / 122 R ©
RFoxPhotography / 124, 136 © Mireille Vautier / 129 © Danita Delimont / 139 L © Beren Patterson / 139 T © John
Warburton-Lee Photography / 141 © Nathan Benn / 147 © Art Directors & TRIP / 149 © Classic Image / 150, 176 ©
Robert Harding Picture Library Ltd / 158 © Doug Steley C / 160 L © Dennis Cox / 160 R © Chao-Yang Chan / 164
© Images & Stories / 173 © Japan Art Collection (JAC) / 183 © Christa Knijff / 185 © LOOK Die Bildagentur der
Fotografen GmbH / 187 © Chile DesConocido. **TopFoto:** 83, 121 © Fortean / 103, 108 , 152, 153, 155, 157, 180 L ©
The Granger Collection / 111 © Hal Beral / 127 © TopFoto / 163 © Charles Walker / 177 © Svensson/Fortean.

This edition published in 2015 by
Chartwell Books
an imprint of Book Sales
a division of Quarto Publishing Group USA Inc.
142 West 36th Street, 4th Floor
New York, New York 10018
USA

ISBN-13: 978-0-7858-3336-9

Printed in China